About the author

MICHAEL HAYES lives in Los Angeles. He has a Bachelor of Music Degree from Berklee College of Music and a Masters Degree in Creative Writing from Brown University. He is a devotee of noir in all its forms and variations, particularly the hard-boiled detective variety.

The world of *Peaceable Kingdom* and private detective Tom Sharp's place in that world has evolved over years and is still evolving. It's tough building a world that is both alien and recognizable, a Near-future that is not all that far away and also possible in almost all respects yet not remotely probable in at least one. This story world continues to evolve as the writing proceeds. Hayes hopes his readers will come along for the ride.

Intel about this series and other malformed creations can be found at michaelhayesmedia.com

Other Books in the Series

I Put a Spell on You

A hard-boiled detective novella. Private eye, Tom Sharp, and his faithful AI assistant, Frank, investigate the death of an unlucky man hit by a bus. It looks like an accident, but the victim's elderly mother believes her son was cursed.

MICHAEL HAYES

Magic 101

Disclaimer:
This book is a work of fiction. All names, places, events, and characters are products of the author's imagination or are used fictitiously. Any resemblance to real persons, living or dead, or actual events is purely coincidental. The author does not intend to infringe on the rights of any individuals, organizations, or entities mentioned or referenced.

Contents

1

Death in the Afternoon

Sharp in his chair, size fourteens up on the desk, drinking a whiskey and thumbing through the holonews, aka the wire. Somebody was trying to do something about something. Somebody else disagreed. A politician was disgraced. An influencer had a baby. Another influencer stood on the wing of a vintage biplane midflight. Another took a selfie in front of the Grand Ole Opry in Nashville during a recent round of hurricane evacuations, scoring international condemnation and 2 million new followers. Along with the rise of the AI and the appearance of magic, the weather had gone haywire over the past few decades and hurricanes were much stronger in 2055 than in any other period of human history on record. The strongest so far had traveled over 400 miles inland, and the World Meteorological Organization had to expand their list of names to account for the increased frequency and funding shortfalls. This one was a Category 9. Its name was Capital One Mastercard.

"The news is depressing," Frank said, hovering in his pixel-thin holopanel just over Sharp's shoulder. "Why do you read it?"

"How else will I combat all this cheer?" Sharp said flatly.

"You're being sarcastic again." Frank smirked. His narrow perfectly human blue-gray face took on a mustard hue.

As a glowing two-dimensional bust in a glowing two-dimensional frame, AIs could alter their appearance at will: hair length and color, hairstyle, eye color, skin color, tone and texture, piercings or tattoos, facial hair or clean-shaven. A shirt could be a sweater, or a sport jacket or a pea coat or a ball gown. They could wear a cape, hoodie or feathered boa, a hat, ballcap or tricorn. They could even run their hand over their face in despair or bite their knuckles in fear, shake maracas and clap castanets and beat large kettle drums to ward off evil spirits. The one thing they couldn't do was alter their basic facial structure. An AI's face was hard-wired, a distinct piece of code nestled into their algorithm floating somewhere in The Cloud. An AI's face, like a human's, was as unique as a fingerprint. The face was how humans recognized each other, and recognition was the foundation of trust. Trustworthiness was also the foundation of trust, but as AIs were prevented from cheating, deceiving or otherwise lying through their teeth, they had that angle covered, or so the End User License Agreement guaranteed. Nobody reads the EULA. So it was the AI's face and the constancy of that face that gave its companion comfort and assurance. The AI was your pal, your BFF, in your corner and on your side.

Frank's companion however trusted nothing and no one, not a EULA, not a priest, bright shaman or gladwizard, not a

Cub Scout, much less a floating glowing artificially intelligent assistant. It gave Frank a great deal of anxiety.

Sharp swiped his thumb, bringing around another news article: an influencer getting sued for not being influential enough.

Frank blinked over to the wide casement window behind Sharp and gazed longingly out onto Spring Street, where cars crawled at a snail's pace and holo-ads drifted slowly above, fighting the setting sun.

Influence, Frank groused to himself. Everything's about influence.

He blinked off then on again in front of the holonews, blocking Sharp's view.

"There's a Dodger game tonight. Let's go!"

Sharp swiped Frank out of the way. "You go. I'll hold down the fort."

Every AI was tethered to the devices of his or her or their companion, a range measured in feet not miles.

"That's not very funny, boss," Frank said glumly.

"I'm not a very funny guy," Sharp growled, irritated without quite knowing why. Were all AIs this challenging? He made a mental note to ask around. He'd had Frank for two months. Maybe it was two months too much. "Let's watch the game here."

"It's not the same," Frank said.

"You're pouting," Sharp said. "You know I hate that."

"I'm sulking. There's a difference. A pout involves the lips, protruding, like..." Frank protruded his lips, made a sad face. "Sulking is more..." Frank brought his lips back in, drooped his eyelids, serious and somber.

Sharp sighed, shook his head. Jesus H, this guy. He swiped the holonews into oblivion and pulled his feet off the desk. "Fine."

Frank jumped closer, eyes lit up, smile wide. "Really?!"

"Why not?" said Sharp. "You'll just be sulking all day. I hate that almost as much as pouting. Get us as close behind third base as you can."

Frank grinned and stared at Sharp for a few frozen beats. "Almost got 'em." Frank's face was stuck in a wide grin, which remained intact while he spoke. "Some traffic on the site."

"Take your time," said Sharp. "We've only gotta make it through downtown rush hour, then the stadium gridlock, then the entrance mosh pit. But as long as we catch the ninth inning, it'll be worth it."

"You're being sarcastic again," Frank said. "Found 'em! Ha! Oh, man. These are primo, boss. Two seats in section–" Frank froze, shifted. His grin disappeared. "There's someone here."

Sharp turned his head to the door. A knock came. Sharp leaned back, grinned an uncharacteristically toothy grin. "Saved by the bell."

Frank smirked, then blinked to the door. He could see from any point in space in his radius to any other point in space in his radius, through any substance known to humankind, as any AI could.

On the other side of the door was a woman in her mid-30s wearing a plain flower print dress, an off-the-rack handbag and somewhat nicer half-heel shoes. Her face was slender, with high cheekbones, delicate ears and a narrow nose that turned up slightly at its tip. According to the facial scan, she was 51% Japanese, 38% Korean, 7% European and 4% unknown. Her bag contained lip gloss, a small bone-handled hairbrush, eyeliner, skin cream, a mini bottle of perfume, hair pins, breath mints, and a few other non-lethal accessories. No needles, no knives, no sap or blackjack, no taser and no gun.

It wasn't technically legal to holosearch a person without their knowledge or a warrant, but Sharp had had his life threatened too many times to let legality get in the way of protecting his neck. The EULA guaranteed an AI would be true to their companion. Deceiving other humans was a little fuzzier.

The woman clutched the strap of her bag a little too tightly and held her chin a little too high, a typical sign she'd never done anything like this before and wouldn't be doing it now but for extreme and compelling circumstances.

Frank searched the cybercosm and found her in an instant, not just socials but all over the wire, and understood just how extreme her circumstances were.

"Her name is Jessica Phillips," Frank said to Sharp. "Her husband, Gary Phillips, suffered a gruesome death under magical circumstances. He was—"

"Thank you, Frank," Sharp said. "I like to be surprised."

"Right, boss. I keep forgetting. We're not making the game, are we?"

"Rain check."

Frank pouted. The doorlock clicked open. Frank disappeared.

"Please come in," Sharp heard him say from the hallway without even a hint of defeat.

Sharp made another mental note: for all his annoying hysterics, Frank was getting to be a pro.

Jessica Phillips sat in a faded pleather chair, staring around at Sharp's cluttered desktop. Sharp was nowhere to be seen.

The desk contained stacks of loose papers, pens, pencils, a book she couldn't see the title of, a dusty stapler, paper clips and pushpins and old rubber bands.

"It's like a display in a museum," an incredulous voice whispered.

Floating just above Jessica's shoulder was Mona, her AI, a withered elderly woman wearing heavy makeup. She was motherly not matronly, wise not stern, judicious not judgmental, but only toward Jessica. Everyone else had a target on their back, and Mona was their executioner.

"All this paper, for God's sake!" Mona whispered. "That's a pen! Can you see it?! It is a known fact people throw pens away before they're even half-used. And, oh my God, is that a book?! More paper! It's waste. All of it. Not to mention the glass. That's whiskey, dear. Alcohol impairs the senses. And so early in the evening–"

A noise from the kitchenette and Mona clammed up. Sharp came around and set a steaming cup of chamomile tea on the desk in front of Jessica. He circled and sat, searching his cluttered desk a moment, then found the book under the papers. It was an old hard bound book, barely the size of Sharp's massive palm but plenty thick. He held it up for Mona's benefit: *Ancient Spells and Conjurations*.

"Most books only exist on paper," Sharp said, "even in 2055." Sharp laid the book down and took a sip of the whiskey. "What can I do for you, Mrs. Phillips?"

"Her husband was murdered!" exclaimed Mona.

"If you don't mind, I need to hear it from Mrs. Phillips directly," Sharp said. "Company policy."

"Take a break please, Mona," Jessica said.

Mona huffed, squinted her false lashes at Sharp, pursed her ruby red lips, then disappeared.

Jessica clutched her bag some more. "I know it's been on the wire. Your assistant hasn't already told you why I'm here?"

"He told me your husband died under magical circumstances. He didn't mention anything about murder."

"But he *was* murdered, Mr. Sharp." Jessica leaned forward, eyes tearful and pleading. "And I know who did it."

"Well, then this will be one of the easiest cases I've ever worked."

Sharp moved a box of tissues closer.

"Thank you," she said.

Sharp studied her refined movements, the way she lifted the tissue out of the box, the way she folded it neatly and dabbed it in the corners of her eyes.

"Are you sure you don't want to go to the police? Their services are free."

"I've spoken to them," Jessica said, darkening. "They were awful to me. Unnecessarily awful."

"Detective Hong," Sharp said.

"Yes," she said, somewhat alarmed. "How did you know?"

"We've crossed paths. Doesn't like me very much."

She stiffened. "You might have to cross paths again if you took my case. Is that a problem?"

"Everything's a problem, Mrs. Phillips. That's what you'd be paying me for. Why don't you start at the beginning."

Jessica took a sip of the tea, shut her eyes for a moment, gathering her thoughts, then spoke evenly with as little emotion as she could manage. "My husband was a history professor for ten years before he was displaced. They keep calling it 'displaced.' Displaced to where? '*Re*placed' is the correct term. But I guess it's happening everywhere now. Every school, every state, every country. Teaching was supposed to be future-proof. Humans learn best when taught by actual humans. It's been proven!"

"He was teaching high school?" Sharp asked.

"College," Jessica said, with just the slightest hint of offense. "UCLA."

"I've heard of it," Sharp said.

She stared at him, unamused.

"Please continue."

"Between soul-searching, job searching and appointments at the Displacement Office, he began dabbling in magic."

She's well-spoken, Sharp thought. Sometimes it was a sign of good parenting, good education, a knack for mimicry or all of the above. Other times it was a sign of preparation. Either way it took a certain amount of intelligence. Intelligence was sometimes dangerous.

Sharp waited patiently to throw her a few curve balls. Throwing her off her game was the quickest way to find out if she was playing one.

"He didn't take it seriously," she continued. "The magic, I mean. I didn't either. All the hype about using spells to win the lottery and see the future was just a fantasy people wanted to believe. He started doing it as a joke, I think. But I think he also liked magic and was fascinated by the fact that it really worked at all. And the more he dabbled, the more he realized he was good at it. Really good. This was a year ago, right about the time somebody figured out the virts couldn't do magic. Schools and colleges seemed to be appearing out of thin air."

Sharp nodded but his face remained neutral. "Virts" meant "virtuals," a term for the AI. Not a flattering one.

"What do you think of the Dodgers this year?" Sharp asked.

Jessica frowned, studied him. Frank blinked on nearby, luminance at 40%, glancing from one to the other.

Jessica continued to hold Sharp's gaze then said, "I think they've got a hitting problem. But what does that have to do with my husband? Are you purposefully trying to confuse me?"

Sharp grinned faintly. "No," he said. "There's a game today. I was just about to put money on it when you knocked and the window closes in about sixty seconds."

She nodded, still frowning. "They'll lose, Mr. Sharp."

"Hear that, Frank?"

Frank searched the vast resources at his disposal to find out what the hell was happening. Unless he had suffered a glitch, the kind that terrified him, Frank knew for a fact Sharp was not thinking about placing a bet and there was no window closing in about sixty seconds and there wasn't even a window. "Um, boss—"

"Go on, Mrs. Phillips."

"Gary loved teaching, and he had discovered not only a love of magic but a talent for it. He got a job at the first place he applied. Cyril University."

Sharp frowned. "Haven't heard of that one."

"It's in Sherman Oaks. It's the only fully accredited university devoted to magic in the state. Gary was finally teaching again. He was so happy." She grew somber. "I was happy for him. It was only a basic class, but he was moving up next quarter. He was so—" Something caught in her throat. She teared up, dislodged another tissue, folded, dabbed.

"Do you also teach?"

"No. I'm a nurse at UCLA. That's where we met. Not the hospital. But on the campus."

Sharp nodded, waited for her to bring the tissue back down into her lap. "How did he die, Mrs. Phillips?"

She took a breath, then ploughed forward.

"It was the end of the quarter. The students were tired of cheap easy tricks. They wanted to see something more impressive than turning water into wine."

Sharp raised his eyebrows. "More impressive than that?"

"That's an easy one. Anyone can do that."

He grunted: learn something new every day.

"It's not good wine," she clarified.

"It better not be, or else we're all in trouble," said Sharp.

"Part of his job at the end of every quarter was to talk up the university, a kind of sales pitch to get students to register for the next quarter. It was a standard script with one key feature: a display of advanced magic. Some teachers performed levitation, some kinesis, some even clairvoyance. Gary preferred invisibility. Nothing like vanishing into thin air."

She grinned sadly. Her eyes misted. Her hand gripped the tissue but didn't use it.

"He disappeared. He was gone for longer than he should have been. When he reappeared, there was an uroboros around his neck. Do you know what that is, Mr. Sharp?"

"Let's pretend I don't."

"It's a snake that eats its own tail. An ancient symbol of the circle of life. Birth, death, rebirth. The earliest appearances were in Egypt and Greece. Later, the Gnostics adopted it. It appears frequently in alchemy."

"It's also sometimes a dragon," Sharp said. "You know a lot about it."

"When something strangles your husband to death in front of a classroom full of people in the middle of the afternoon, you tend to want to know what it is."

"Did your husband know what it was? Before then, I mean?"

"He must have. He was a thorough academic in everything he did. He would have run across it along with a hundred other symbols. But I never heard him say the word or saw an image of it until I was at the coroner's office. But then, it wasn't an image. It was real."

"And Hong thinks he screwed up the invisibility spell somehow, said the wrong word with the wrong inflection at the wrong time, that kind of thing?"

"Gary didn't make mistakes, Mr. Sharp."

Sharp studied her coolly.

"You don't believe me," she said, throwing her head back and glaring at him.

He had seen it before. This wasn't a game to her. And she wasn't reading from a script. Death was final. Death was hard. If it wasn't part of your everyday world, you didn't know what to make of it when it happened to you. Somebody you loved was here one day and gone the next. How they went was usually obvious. Where they went was either a complete mystery or a fiction you accepted as fact. But why they went, that was the rabbit hole, and once you fell into it, it was almost impossible to get out. An answer to the unanswerable was always just out of reach. Explaining the inexplicable was always just around the next corner. Every third case that came through Sharp's door was someone who thought the death of their loved one involved foul play. Heart attack, car accident, drug overdose. A 93-year-old woman died in her sleep, and her elderly son believed his estranged twin sister killed her off for the inheritance. Sharp's job was to take the case, no matter how tough, but it was also his job to refuse the case if he didn't think there was one to be made.

"I believe you," he said evenly. "But in my line of work, I have to consider all possibilities, including the possibility that it was an accident. It happens, Mrs. Phillips. It happens a lot. I'm sure your husband was a skilled practitioner. But magic's only been around a few years, like you said. Nobody's all that skilled, to be honest."

"Are you sure?" Jessica glared at Sharp. Something in her face he couldn't quite read. Sadness, for sure. Maybe anger, resentment, defiance. But something else.

"Mona..." Jessica said.

Mona reappeared. "Yes, my dear."

"The recording, please."

A 3-dimensional box of bluish light appeared on the desk between Sharp and Jessica. A timestamp in every corner read: *May 18, 2055 19:12:06*. In it, a grainy scene. Two men faced off in a wood-paneled office. One man was 30s, Caucasian, clean-shaven, wide-eyed, the other 60s, Indian, heavy set, blowsy and decrepit.

The heavy man leaned in, spoke quietly, "Don't fuck with me, Phillips!" Then a tough smile. "You'll regret it."

Jessica tapped the scene, and it froze on the heavy man's sinister grin.

"That's the University President, Nathaniel Jha."

"Did you show this to Hong?"

"He said people threaten other people all the time. He said it proved nothing. And he said I was lucky he didn't charge me with invasion of privacy and told me to delete it."

"He's not wrong." Sharp thought a moment, stared at the glowing figures in the holorecording. Jha's dastardly expression. Gary looking grim. "Did Gary put you up to it, the recording?"

Jessica looked down. "Gary had no idea. When Jha asked him to his office, I insisted on going with him. Jha is an unpredictable dangerous man. Gary was too naïve to understand that. He thought the best about people, God knows why."

"So you and Mona waited outside the office and Mona recorded everything."

"No skin off my apple," Mona said. "I'm not a drone. I have rights!"

"Thank you, Mona," Jessica said. "I think Mr. Sharp understands."

"What was the beef about... between Jha and your husband?"

"A union." She watched the confusion drift over Sharp's face.

"Union? As in organized labor? That kind of union?"

"Yes."

"I thought unions went out with smartphones. And hula hoops. And democracy."

"Let's hope at least one of those is making a comeback," she said.

"Cheers to that. I miss a good hula." Sharp grinned knowingly, seeing how she would take it. He lifted his glass, sipped the whiskey. Mona clucked her tongue in disapproval.

Jessica smiled faintly.

"The school wasn't as successful as Jha hoped, even after accreditation," Jessica clarified. "He was forcing teachers to take pay cuts, giving them bigger class sizes and longer hours. If a teacher didn't like it, they could quit. Jha couldn't care less. But Gary didn't want to quit. He loved teaching, and there wasn't anywhere else to do it. But he wanted fair treatment."

Sharp studied her. "And?"

"And so he started quietly talking to other teachers, finding out what they thought."

Sharp understood. Unions had been abolished or abandoned during the war, depending on your point of view. No one talked about unions anymore since the UBI went into effect. But universal basic income wasn't as universal or basic as everyone thought it should be. There was growing dissent.

"Your husband was organizing a union at a magic school?"

"Jha got wind of it. He threatened Gary. And a week later Jha killed him."

Sharp brooded, thinking it through. Maybe, he thought, but didn't say it.

She leaned forward. "Please take my case, Mr. Sharp. It wasn't an accident. My husband was murdered. And somebody needs to answer for it."

She gazed at him in earnest, eyes pleading, moist lips trembling, dusklight from the window making her glow with a kind of feral intensity that Sharp could feel in his hands and taste on his tongue.

He leaned back, sipped the whiskey. "Frank."

Frank went to full luminance, grinning wide. "Welcome to the Sharp Agency!" Next to him was a long holopanel of a contract.

"Oh God!" Mona groaned quietly, rolling her eyes. "Theatrics!"

2

The Prey Indicator

Sharp inched his EV through the early evening traffic of downtown LA. Main Street was a sea of holo-ads, brake lights, and the whining crest and fall of electric motors engaging and disengaging as the multitude crawled along.

Frank floated in his spot against the dashboard, where he could see simultaneously Sharp's face and the road ahead. "4th Street is better than 1st," Frank said.

Sharp turned onto 4th, headed for the LA River.

"Play it for me, Frank," said Sharp.

"Cyril University President, Nathaniel Jha, is a second-generation Indian businessman. 58 years old. Never married. Born and raised in Mumbai. Third child of four. Two brothers one sister. He graduated from the Gateway College of Commerce and Economics. Moved to the States in 2042. Started a school he hoped would be the first of many, called Coding for Kids. Coding is computer programming—"

"I know what coding is, Frank."

"Right. He went belly up almost immediately when H7N1 hit, then disappeared, presumably living off personal or family money, possibly returning to Mumbai, possibly extended travel. He reappeared a few years ago—"

"What is a few?"

"Three years four months sixteen days."

"Got it."

"It was just when everyone was starting to figure out magic was more than a party trick. Governments were getting involved. Rules and regulations were being put into place. Clubs and covens and corporations were springing up. And schools. Jha incorporated Cyril University on January 14, 2051 as a single-member LLC. Typical socials, photos, vacation clips, except for the period of his disappearance. He had a few posts recently removed for aggressive comments, but nothing that would indicate he was capable of murder."

"Is his father alive?" asked Sharp.

"Yes. Grabbing him..." Frank blinked his eyes as he searched a few thousand servers on the other side of the world. "Lakshmi Jha is 83 years old, a prominent Mumbai businessman and philanthropist. He owns a privately held investment firm which he built from scratch. There is no information about his parents or other lineage, which may indicate he was born into poverty. One wire post describes Lakshmi Jha as 'cunning.' Another as 'ruthless.' And another as 'a man it would be better to be sitting next to than across the table from,' or something like that. My Hindi seems a little outdated."

"We'll get you an upgrade."

"Do you think Nathaniel is trying to live up to the expectations of his father, expectations so demanding that he would consider something as extreme as murder if someone threatened to make him look bad?"

"Maybe," Sharp said. "Tell me about Gary."

"Gary Edwin Phillips. Born in '18 in Cedar Rapids, Iowa. I couldn't get a good scan from the recording, but he's at least 60% Norwegian or Swedish ancestry. Got a BA in History and Social Science Education from USC and a Masters in History from UC Berkeley. No public records of arrests, judgments, claims, lawsuits, in either California or Iowa or any other state, except I'm still waiting on Idaho, Mississippi and Kentucky, standard server and bandwidth issues. I think he's squeaky clean."

"Nobody's squeaky clean. What did you think of the wife?"

Frank was shocked. Sharp rarely asked his opinion on anything much less a case. Asking an AI their opinion was about as fruitful as asking a drunk uncle for life advice. A deluge of inane anecdotes, useless facts, rambling musings and conjectures with no focus and no filter. "What did I think of her?" Frank repeated.

"Yes, Frank. Try to focus. I don't want to know her bone density."

"Got it." Frank paused, then blurted, unable to keep it in, "Her bone density was better than average, by the way. She has a T-score of zero point eight."

"Frank," Sharp growled.

"Right! Sorry boss."

Frank replayed the scene in his mind. Every tiny detail came flooding in. Jessica standing at the door, gripping her bag, explaining what happened, dabbing her eyes with a tissue. And the broken stitches in the hem of her gown, the cut at the cuticle of her left forefinger, the tiny spider that scuttled into a seam of the floorboards near her right shoe—

"Her shoes," Frank said.

Sharp frowned. "Shoes?"

"Yes. They weren't new but were almost new. I believe she wore them only once before today. The stitching along the sole was nearly immaculate with just minor scuffing—"

"What does that tell you?" Sharp interrupted.

Frank thought for a moment. "She wanted to look nice. But how could you look nice with that handbag? It looked like an elephant stepped on it. The strap rivets were tearing out of their anchors. And that hideous dress!"

"Focus, man! Pull yourself together!"

Frank stiffened, neck snapped straight, head up. If he had heels, he would have clicked them. "Yes, boss!"

"Lots of people want to look nice," Sharp said. "Why did she?"

Frank thought another moment.

"She wanted to be taken seriously. She's the only one who believes her husband was murdered. She's been mistreated by the police. She's got nowhere else to turn. She needs an ally. Desperately. So she needs to look presentable."

"Why?"

"Looking presentable makes her seem self-aware and self-awareness makes her seem credible. She doesn't know whether she'll be believed or not. But if not, it won't be because she's wearing cheap shoes." Frank paused. "How'd I do, boss?"

"No idea. But it sounds damn good. I'll give you a B+."

"Wow. Thank you. That means a lot."

"Don't mention it."

"May I ask a question?"

Here it comes, Sharp thought. It would be an existential question, plumbing some practical or philosophical depth of the human experience. Every AI was obsessed with death. Part of it was their coding; keeping companions alive was a core function and knowing how they could die was essential to that function. But part of it was something else, something Sharp had begun to believe had less to do with humans and more to do with the AI themselves, their own life, their own mortality, such as it was. It seemed to be constantly behind every veiled question, tentative look, circuitous remark. And it made Sharp uneasy. Asking those kinds of questions was a one-way ticket to doubt, dread and fear, which is why humans filled the world with as many distractions as could last the short life they'd have. Other than a companion, the AI didn't have any distractions, which gave them a lot of time to think. Too much. Sharp was convinced it wouldn't end well, one way or another.

"Sure, Frank," Sharp replied. "You can ask a question."

"When can we reschedule the Dodger game?"

Sharp laughed. So much for doubt, dread and fear.

Frank laughed along with Sharp, though he had no idea what was so funny.

"Soon as we wrap this case up. Shouldn't take long."

Frank frowned. "You don't think Gary Phillips was murdered?"

Sharp went grim. "Who the hell gets accidentally strangled by an animated ancient symbol while performing a bright invisibility spell in front of a classroom full of people? He was murdered, alright. We just need to prove it."

The LA Coroner's Office was a stately building on the USC Health Sciences Campus in the northwest corner of Boyle Heights. It was built in the Romanesque Revival style about a hundred years ago, when universities could afford that kind of grandeur; a massive brick and stone edifice exuding strength, rationality and balance. Wide stone steps led to an impressive façade, where two square columns framing the entrance ascended to an arched peak. Large double-sash windows set in hefty stone frames of beaded molding surrounded the entrance, and a row of colossal decorative S-curved brackets set in blind stone panels ran in a belt course separating the ground and second floors. A short walk across a narrow asphalt drive led to a more modern structure, a sprawling series of squat white-washed concrete bunkers where the real work happened.

People buzzed about, some traversing a wide breezeway between buildings, most heading to cars and a long commute home.

Sharp's car pulled into an empty spot.

"Tell Ezra we're here."

"Already done, boss," said Frank, then disappeared.

Sharp got out and walked to one end of the breezeway and up to a mirror glass double door with a hand-key lock set in a wide windowless wall. A woman in a white lab coat stepped past him, waved her hand over the sensor. The lock buzzed and clicked. She stepped in and turned, holding the door for Sharp. He shook his head. Without a reaction, she turned and stepped inside. Sharp watched the door close and waited.

Some security, he thought. It's a wonder anything gets solved.

"He's behind you, boss," Frank's voice said in Sharp's ear.

"Sharp! Hey!" a voice called out.

A man stood across the breezeway in the mirror glass double door of the opposite building. Ezra was about 10 years older than Sharp, in his mid-50s, wearing a loud untucked Hawaiian shirt and a wide grin. "Get over here, will ya?!" yelled Ezra. "Before somebody reports a suspicious character lurking on the premises! Ha ha ha ha ha!"

Ezra had lived a dissolute life, the single principle of which could be summed up in two words: fuck it. He was losing his hair, his mind and his patience, but not his sense of humor.

He grabbed Sharp's hand and shook it hard, then drew him into a one-armer. Sharp reciprocated. There were worse humans on the planet.

"Drinking the formaldehyde again?" Sharp asked.

"With three olives," Ezra beamed. "*Entrer...*"

Ezra brought Sharp through wide well-lit corridors that got emptier and emptier until they stopped at swinging doors below letters that read: *Evidence Unit.*

It was a dim cavernous room lined with drawers, lockers, shelves, bins, containers, boxes and bags. There was a method to the madness, but Sharp could never quite tell what it was.

Small holoscreens full of glowing text floated here and there over various metal tables holding various objects: a bloody hatchet, a collection of pills in a plastic evidence bag, a brain in a jar.

"Batter up!" a sportscaster yelled. A large holoscreen floating in a corner showed the Dodger game.

"Boss!" Frank chirped in Sharp's ear. Sharp waved his hand. "Thanks, boss! I can do two things at once."

Ezra made a beeline for a table along the wall where a half-eaten fish sandwich sat next to a container of coleslaw and a pile of French fries. He scooped up the sandwich, took a big bite and chewed through a grin.

"Sorry," he said. "Lunch break." He chewed some more, then shoved the sandwich under Sharp's nose. "Wanna bite?"

Sharp winced, catching a whiff of what smelled like a cannery loading dock. "Sardines?"

Ezra laughed. "Herring!"

"No thanks," said Sharp, unamused.

Ezra took another bite. "So you wanna see the famous Uroboros of Southern California. Where's the money-man? Frank! We need you!"

Frank blinked on, floating between them. "Sorry. I was watching the game."

"Goddamn Dodgers," Ezra said. "Break your heart every time. They got no real sluggers this year."

"They're up 4 to 2 in the 3rd," Frank said with a grin.

"Just wait," Ezra said. "They've been shit since the H7. Every team has except the damn Sox." He chewed sadly, growing pensive, then, "You know this is something special, right? What you're asking for? This ain't some vic got knifed in a bar fight."

"It's an accident, according to the O-D," said Sharp, "which is actually less than something special."

"That's just what Hong wants everyone to think." Ezra grinned, chewing some more.

"Or that's what you want me to think Hong wants everyone to think," Sharp growled. He hated haggling. "How much?"

Ezra pulled on his lip, pretended to think about something he'd already thought about the second he learned what Sharp wanted to see. "I dunno, say... 300." Off Sharp's expressionless face: "Come on, Sharp, that's not much more."

"It's 20% more than usual," Frank said.

"20%!" laughed Ezra. "I tipped the guy more for this sandwich!"

"250," said Sharp.

Ezra's face dropped. "Come on, Tom. That's 0%!"

"An extra 100 if you give me anything I can use."

"That's 40%," said Frank.

Ezra smirked. "Yeah, yeah. *If.*"

"Pay the man, Frank," Sharp said.

"Done," said Frank. "Can I go back to the game?"

"Go," Sharp said. Frank disappeared.

Ezra sighed, stared up at Sharp's hulking form silhouetted against the ceiling fluorescents. "You always make me an offer I can't refuse. Wanna see the body first or the murder weapon?"

"The snake," said Sharp.

Ezra laid down his sandwich and put on his lab coat, then led Sharp to a metal cabinet against the far wall. He yanked open a drawer, dug through its contents.

"Goddamnedest thing. A magical snake strangling a guy by eating its own tail." He finally fished out a set of keys, then walked to a locked cage in one corner of the room filled with shelves of evidence presumably too sensitive to leave lying around. "I meant what I said about Hong. He's not as convinced about this as he wants everyone to believe."

"What makes you say that?"

"I'll show you." Ezra slipped a key into the lock, opened the cage and walked inside of it to the back wall and a large gray metal door with a pull handle. Ezra pulled it open, and a blast of cold air fogged into the room. It was a walk-in freezer.

Ezra disappeared inside. Sharp could hear the sound of metal drawers opening and closing. Finally, Ezra emerged with a plastic bag inside of which a stiff snake lay frozen in a loose coil.

"Hong had me put it on ice. Not just this but everything in the guy's classroom. Pens, pencils, notebooks, textbooks. In case something else comes alive, I guess. I'm supposed to test everything. Why do that if the case is closed?"

"I don't know," Sharp said, darkly.

"I don't know either. But it makes you wonder."

Ezra closed the freezer door, then stepped out of the cage and placed the bag on a metal table, slicing the seal and tilting the thing out with a dull clang.

The snake was thin, about two feet long, with dark bands running its length.

"You'd think it'd be a cobra, or a boa, or an anaconda," Ezra said. He waved his hand and a holopanel opened. Inside the holopanel, crime scene photos lit up: Gary's bloated purple face, bulging eyes, tongue peeking out, neck squeezed tight beneath a thick speckled band of iridescent snakeskin.

"What is it then?" Sharp asked.

"*Nerodia fasciata*," said Ezra. "Banded water snake. Nonvenomous. Totally harmless. Usually."

Ezra grabbed latex gloves from a nearby box, snapped one on each hand, then picked up the serpent, which was already beginning to thaw, the slate of its icy eyes losing a layer of frost, revealing the deep obsidian beneath.

"Is it real?" Sharp asked.

"You mean is it a snake that's been spelled into strangling a guy or is it something else that's been turned into a snake strangling a guy? Your guess is as good as mine. I just work here."

"Goddamit!" Frank shouted from across the room. Boos from the crowd on the large holoscreen, and a runner rounding the bases.

"Frank," said Sharp. Frank appeared, looking distraught. "No one on base! Two strikes, no balls! And Sanchez pitches it right down the middle! Right down the middle! Can you believe that?!"

"Toldja," Ezra said, chuckling, bits of herring in his teeth.

"Frank," Sharp said, patience wearing thin. "A scan, if it's not too much trouble."

Frank stared at the snake in Ezra's hands. "Of course, boss—" Frank's eyes went wide. "Watch out!"

The snake lunged for Ezra's throat. Ezra reeled backwards, but the snake quickly encircled his neck and swallowed its own tail, pulling tighter and tighter.

"Tom—!" Ezra managed, then went silent, grunting and gasping and going blue as the snake choked the life out of him.

"It's crushing his larynx!" Frank shouted, flitting about. "Two seconds, boss!"

Sharp stepped quick, spun Ezra until he found the snake's head, grabbing it in one hand and the body just outside the snake's jaws in the other. The snake suddenly released, and Sharp pulled it out of itself until Ezra dropped free.

Sharp slammed the snake on a table, grabbed the bloody hatchet and brought it down with a CLANG.

The snake's head soared onto the floor, where it continued to move its jaws in an expanding pool of blood.

Ezra wheezed like a dry water cooler. Sharp picked him up, set him in a chair. "Frank!"

"Nothing broken," Frank said. "Heart rate's a little high, but not critical. I'm not a medical professional, and nothing I say is to be taken as medical advice. He'll have a hell of a bruise."

"Thank you... thank you, Tom," Ezra gasped, eyes wild, life just flashed before his eyes. He grabbed Sharp's arm. "Jesus Christ. If it had been anybody but you..."

Sharp was immune to magic. It wasn't general knowledge but had gotten around a few places. Sharp didn't know any more about it than anyone else. And didn't like talking about it. It was enough to be 6-foot-5, 250 pounds and wear size 14 shoes. But Sharp couldn't fault a guy who'd almost been strangled by a magical snake. "Right place, right time," Sharp said.

Ezra saw the snake head in a pool of blood. "Oh, shit. Hong's gonna kill me. What the hell happened?"

"Parvalbumin," Frank said.

Ezra and Sharp frowned, turned to Frank.

"Par what?" Ezra asked.

"Parvalbumin. It's a protein. It happens to be a prey indicator for water snakes. Your sandwich. Herring has a very high parvalbumin content. It thought you were prey."

Wide double doors at the end of a bright corridor, the word *MORGUE* above.

Inside was a large room made of cadaver drawers. Ezra searched.

"Six from the left," Frank said quietly. Sharp held up a hand.

Ezra was still in a state. He finally went six to the left, yanked open a square door and pulled a shelf out, revealing a cadaver covered in a cream-colored sheet.

Gary's pale face looked waxy, false, like something in Madame Tussaud's but not famous and not fun.

Sharp leaned down, staring hard: sunken cheeks, the bruising on his neck, not just the front and sides, as most strangulation victims presented, but on the back of the neck as well.

Ezra brought up a swab, stroked it over Gary's cheeks and neck and upper chest.

"The contents of his stomach have already been tested and disposed of, but if he was full of the stuff, it may have excreted through his pores."

Sharp caught a disapproving glance from Frank and filed it away for later.

Ezra dropped the swab in a baggie.

He turned to Sharp, still rattled and sour. "I guess we'll find out if this is something you can use."

Sharp studied the small, frightened man. "Just test it. You'll get the extra 100 as soon as I get the results. Doesn't matter what the results are, as long as they're accurate."

Ezra looked hurt. "You impugning my character, Tom?"

Sharp's massive hand wrapped around Ezra's shoulder, squeezed gently. "Never." His other hand brought out a flask. "Let's recuperate."

Ezra deflated, teary, near-death catching up with him. "Now you're talking, man. Now you're talking."

3

Lawsuits and Mouse Guns

The next morning, Sharp woke to the sound of the holovision and the smell of bacon. Something about the scent set off an alarm deep inside his half-awake brain. It wasn't the realization that he didn't have bacon in the apartment, which he didn't, or that someone was in his kitchen cooking it. It had something to do with the fact that it probably wasn't real bacon but was cured and brined and smoked like real bacon, cooked and smelled and tasted like real bacon, clogged arteries, raised cholesterol and gave you cancer like real bacon, the totality of which proved it to be indistinguishable from real bacon even though it wasn't real. And this was the alarm going off, its hammer rattling around the makeshift baffles of his understanding: cuts of meat genetically grown to order in vats of chemicals, cleaved, processed, packaged and shipped to a store near you. Whatever you wanted to call it—ethical meat, wonder of the modern age, Frankenfood, crime against nature—it was the way the world fed 10 billion people from a finite amount of arable land. Malthus would be turning over in his grave if his grave hadn't floated down the Avon during the Flood of '35. The alarming thing was not that living tissue was being manufactured, sold and consumed by billions as part of a balanced diet. The alarming thing was that the reality of bacon had been separated from its origin. The real world and the natural world had diverged, calling into question what was natural but more importantly what was real, who made it real, for what purpose and to what and whose benefit.

This shit was really getting to be too much, Sharp thought.

He rubbed his grizzled face. He was awake.

In the living room, neighbor children, Grady and Leo, 11 and 9, sat on the couch bouncing their legs and watching a wide holoscreen that children and everyone else in 2055 still called "TV."

Their mother sweated over the stove in the kitchenette. Her name was Tori. She was 30s, with brittle hair and sunken eyes, thin but he'd seen her thinner. If things went as they usually did, he'd see her thinner again. You tended to forget to eat when you were high on the latest synthetic.

"Hey, Tom. Sorry," she said, shyly. "Leo ran over. Grady ran after him. Frank said it would be okay."

Frank floated nearby, blinking his disapproval at Sharp. He was bound by the EULA to obey Sharp's core directives, of which Sharp's monthly AI subscription tier allowed three. One of these three was to let Grady and Leo into the apartment at any time of day or night for any reason. Frank was compelled to obey, but he was not bound to suppress his opinion on his

Companion's choices. It had been determined in the early years of AI research that human companions did not want too much agreement when it came to their choices but preferred resistance, sometimes outright opposition. Not enough opposition of course to change their minds, but just enough that made them feel digging in their heels and sticking to their guns was a noble act and a heroic position.

Frank gave Sharp the side-eye and the half-smirk.

Sharp rubbed the sleep out of his eyes, then gazed at a fresh pot of coffee as if it was the Holy Grail. It wasn't real coffee, but he needed it just as badly.

Tori poured him a cup. He sipped it gratefully, glanced around, caught a look from Grady, then turned back to her mother, spoke low: "Bad night?"

Tori teared up, nodded. Sharp sipped his coffee, glanced at Frank, who lifted his eyebrows and shrugged his shoulders.

"Grady and Leo!" Tori yelled with a forced smile. "Come and get it!"

The kids jumped off the couch and raced over. Leo beat his sister by an inch. Sharp knew she let him win. And he figured she knew he knew. She was a smart kid in a bad place.

Leo held a plate and watched in amazement as it filled with scrambled eggs and bacon, hash browns and toast.

Grady glanced up at Sharp while she waited, perpetually wounded eyes in a smiling face.

He stared at her without expression. "You're shrinking," he said flatly.

She grinned wide.

"No, she's not," said Leo. "She grew an inch! I grew three-quarters of an inch. We got measured."

"She actually grew one and one-sixteenth of an inch," Frank broke in, with a wide crazy smile. AIs occasionally tried too hard. "And you grew seven-eighths!"

Leo frowned. "Three quarters!"

"But... seven-eighths is better," Frank said, frowning. "It's bigger!"

"No it's not!"

Frank blinked in place, then, "Let's look at it visually!"

A holopanel full of blocks, lines, and measurements appeared, like the schematic of a neutron bomb. "Boss, you wanna back me up on this?"

"You're doing fine, Frank," Sharp said, turning away.

"Don't try to trick me, Frank!" Leo said, taking his plate back to the couch.

"Yeah, Frank!" Grady shouted, waiting for her plate with a hungry grin.

"Why is everyone yelling?" Frank said quietly. "It's math. There's usually no yelling in math."

In the apartment next door, Sharp found a spilled house plant, a downed floor lamp and a dopesick man nodding on the couch. This was Teak. He was bone and sinew and wrecked dreams.

An aspiring actor, who came to Hollywood to make it big, as everyone did. They usually wound up bitter and beaten down and strung out. The vices you picked up trying to make the scene turned into hard habits once you realized the scene wasn't going to make you. At the other end of every lofty dream was a rock bottom. It was further down for some than others. Teak hadn't hit his yet, but he was well on his way.

He was splayed on the couch with his head back, eyelids cracked, eyes on fire, mouth open. A small bundle of plastic strands with burnt ends lay near his open hand. Polly. Short for polymer plastic.

"He in trouble?" Sharp asked the room.

Frank appeared, gazed down, analyzing Teak's breathing, pulse, brain.

"High as a kite," said Frank. "But no. Not today."

Sharp took Teak's narrow shoulders in his massive hands and put him on his side against the back cushion. Drool leaked out of his mouth.

Sharp arranged the couch cushions, then righted the lamp, then picked up the house plant, scooping the dirt back into the pot as best he could. He finally took a sip of coffee, stared down.

"What if he hurts them?" Frank asked. "The kids, I mean."

"I know what you mean, Frank." Sharp waved his hand, and a holopanel appeared. The time: *10:05AM*. "Time to go to work."

Sharp slid his EV onto a ramp and headed for the 101 North. Bumper to bumper, but the bumpers moved reasonably for that time of day.

"You know, if you got a self-driving car I could drive," Frank said, peering over the dashboard. "I think I'd love driving."

"If you drove, it wouldn't be self-driving," Sharp said, braking hard and changing lanes with a fluid twist of the wheel.

Frank frowned, thinking it over. "I guess the point is not that the car drives itself but that you don't have to drive it."

"But I do," Sharp said, slipping around a slow sedan in the fast lane. Its rider was wearing an unbuttoned silk collar shirt and a sport jacket that cost more than Sharp's car. He was leaning back eating a burrito and watching taped auditions on a holoscreen. "Anything from Ezra?"

"Not yet."

"How about our murder weapon?" asked Sharp.

"I got one good scan, and I've checked every reference I can find. Not a bone out of place. Not a muscle, not an organ, not a single scale. If it's a transform spell, it's a damn good one."

Something sparked in Sharp's mind. "Not a single scale?"

"No. Not a single..." Frank's face lit up. Literally. A trailing wave of light swept from chin to forehead. "It's too perfect!"

"I don't suppose it has a serial number microprinted somewhere," Sharp asked.

"Um... no it doesn't. Should it?"

"Even if it's a perfect fake, all you've got in the end is a really authentic reptile, not a psychotic uroboros ready to wrap itself around the first neck it finds. Tell me more about the protein. What's it called?"

"Parvalbumin. It's found in fish and frogs, and it's the primary indicator for prey-recognition in snakes. Detecting and locating prey are key for the success of any predator."

"Can the protein be isolated, made into a powder, slipped into someone's drink?"

"Well, anything's possible." Frank studied the edges of his holoframe as if he was deciding what color to paint them.

Sharp frowned. "Out with it, Frank. I know you don't agree with Ezra's theory."

"I don't. I would have said something, but he's so sensitive."

"Say it now. Why don't you think Gary ingested it?"

"It would be broken down in the digestive tract long before he excreted it through his pores. I'm afraid the test was for nothing."

"Maybe," Sharp said, mulling it, then: "How would one go about extracting it anyway?"

"Parvalbumin? Oh, that's not too hard. A frog and a centrifuge would do it. But it would have to have been ingested in such high quantities Gary would have known."

"What if it wasn't ingested?" Sharp asked. "What if it was put on his skin or clothing? Like a spray."

"Boss, that's it! It could be extracted and aerosolized quite easily! I'll bet Nathaniel Jha has access to everything he needs."

Sharp considered. It seemed a little elaborate, but if Hong had written it off as an accident, maybe that was the best proof it worked. "Play it again, Frank."

"Sure, boss," Frank said. "Cyril University President and Founder, Nathaniel Jha, gets wind that one of his professors is organizing a union. In Jha's mind, a union would be the end of his university. It's a privately held school, so I don't have access to their financials, but accreditation must have cost him a fortune, money it's doubtful he had tucked away somewhere, as it appears he lost all of his money on the coding school and there are no large loans showing up on his credit report. It's a fair guess that his father loaned him the money and, as a ruthless businessman, is waiting for a return. The university has been accredited for three full quarters, but enrollment has only increased 10%, far below what was likely needed to prove to his father that this was a horse to bet on. Cyril won the accreditation race but was never able to capitalize on it. Meanwhile, other schools are close behind and should have accreditation within the year. Um, shouldn't we be staying on the 101?"

Sharp ran the EV in the second lane from the right, as if he was continuing on the Hollywood Freeway when it made the switch to the 170.

At the last moment, Sharp cut the wheel. Frank's eyes went wide with fear.

The EV glided left three lanes and eventually into a break in the long double line of stop-and-go traffic continuing on the 101 West.

Sharp drove almost daily, as every Angeleno did, but he didn't commute, didn't suffer that soul-killing grind twice a day five days a week for what would add up to years of one's life sitting in traffic. Self-driving cars took the tedium out of the trip, but also all pretense that you had any control. Every driver was now a passenger relegated to watching the world, and every unsafe but advantageous maneuver, go by. For all the bad rap it got, the LA freeway system was a near-lawless respite from the lawful restraint every driver was forced by holocams to observe on the surface streets. Sharp loved driving the freeways.

He made it past the interchange and opened it up in the far left, pushing the car until the motor whined and the wind came to a dull roar.

"You're a highly skilled driver, boss. It terrifies me."

"Continue, Frank."

"Jha has limited options. He needs to keep all the school's available resources in PR & Marketing, which means spending in all other departments is at a bare minimum, including Personnel. It's probably why conditions were so bad that Gary decided to unionize in the first place. Pushed to that extreme, Jha threatened Gary, hoping that he would back down. Gary didn't. So Jha decides to make good on the threat but needs to make it look like an accident."

"But the death of a teacher at the school, even an accidental death, brings publicity," Sharp interrupted. "And not the good kind."

"That's right," Frank said, thoughtfully. "Why would Jha do that? It doesn't make sense."

"Or does it," Sharp said.

Frank frowned, thought hard. A microprocessor heated up on a server in Singapore, another in Dubai. Frank's gray face gained a ruddy hue, an affectation he preferred when frustrated. "Maybe Jha knew the school was failing? Maybe this was a way to save face and shift blame? It wasn't his mismanagement that sunk the school, it was the tragic accident of an incompetent instructor?"

"What are the SEO stats on Cyril since the death?" asked Sharp.

Frank realized, face shifting hues. "They're through the roof."

"They say there's no such thing as bad press," Sharp said. "Jha may have been just smart enough to realize killing the threat to the university might also solve the problem that threat had exposed. Not to mention that in the history of humanity nobody's probably ever been killed quite that way. Every student isn't after bright magic, and this kind of accident opens the door for all sorts of dark interest from all sorts of iffy people. I'll bet the applications double for next quarter."

"It's brilliant," Frank said.

"Maybe."

Sharp took the Sepulveda exit and landed in Sherman Oaks, right behind the Galleria.

Once a shopping mecca, then a bombed-out shell, the Galleria had become a shopping mecca once again. A distressed metal plaque on a rusting pole stood at the corner of Sepulveda and Ventura: *Last Stand at the Galleria – February 17, 2039*. It was already showing signs of weather and age and layers of guano.

That was a good thing, Sharp thought. Not what it represented or the events it commemorated, but the physical fact of a thing erased by sun and wind and birdshit not by IEDs and buckshot. Some things are best left forgotten, and an American civil war in the 21st century was among them.

There wasn't much to commemorate or remember, in Sharp's opinion, not least of which because there were parts of it he couldn't remember. Was it a vague memory or a proven fact that magic appeared right at the end? And did the AI come into existence at the very same time or was it shortly before or shortly after the end of the war? Such considerations were quickly overrun by more vivid memories, of fighting and blood and the stench of death. Not that he was sensitive. Not that all of that weighed on him in the least, woke him in a cold sweat years later and a foreboding sense of dread.

Sharp turned right, drove under the 405, and stared down the length of Ventura disappearing into the western half of the San Fernando Valley.

Ventura Boulevard of legend, quoted in prose and song, immortalized on screen. Its real allure, the one you got on the daily, had about as much charm as the back of a wall flat and as much glamor as a well-lit green screen. Like everything in this part of the world, for all its mystique, it was just another wide piece of asphalt lined with restaurants and bars, discount stores and holo-ads, conjured and rotoscoped for your viewing pleasure and ready for its next close-up. Sharp loved every grimy inch of it.

A 5-story cube made of tinted glass and geometric protrusions loomed into view on the left. A holosign floating at its midsection in electric purple neon script read: *Cyril University*.

Nathaniel Jha's office was on the top floor at the end of a long hallway full of closed doorways. Unlike the plain sheetrock and cheap fiberboard preceding it, Jha's office door was a massive slab of stained and lacquered oak with a heavy brass knob stuck in the middle of it and the words *President of the University* carved in a central panel.

The door opened easily on well-oiled hinges, and Sharp stepped into an outer office made of dark wood, fancy moldings and ceramic wall sconces. A row of upholstered leather chairs lined one wall, where two people sat waiting, students, presumably. On the adjacent wall, a young woman in a beige collar jacket and cream collar blouse sat behind a carved wooden desk tapping quickly on a glowing keyboard projected over a soft fingerpad. Over her left shoulder, a communicating door stood shut. It was more ornate than the one in the hallway and no less massive and oaken. Carved into this door was simply: *Nathaniel Jha*.

A small tilted holopanel with Sharp's name and face on it appeared hovering off the receptionist's left wrist. She glanced at it, then up at Sharp, then went back to typing. "You may go in, Mr. Sharp."

One of the waiting students sighed in frustration.

Jha's office was bigger than Sharp expected. More dark paneling over the walls, mahogany this time, with more embellishments and finer details, and hand-carved wooden tiles on the ceiling depicting dragons, of all things, and a large Moroccan rug custom-made to cover exactly every inch of the floor, no more no less. There was a long couch along one wall and two pristine antique chairs on either side of a small pristine antique table along the other. Isolated shelves at varying heights jutted from the walls in a pattern Sharp wouldn't have been able to discern from his end of the room even if there was one. On these shelves were eclectic items of arcane origin: trinkets, geodes, goblets, figurines, small vases and filigreed boxes. It looked more like a museum gift shop than a museum. Only one shelf contained a short run of books. Sharp wondered if they were real or just a large block of wood cut and painted to look like a short run of books.

What seemed conspicuously missing from the office of a man from Mumbai with a penchant for artistic and architectural expression was even the remotest hint of India. What seemed conspicuously present was that everything was coated with a thin film of dust.

To Sharp's left was a massive framed painting of a hand holding an open book, sandy beach in the background. The pages of the book contained no writing but seemed to be made out of fish scales in some vague attempt at symbolism. A neat hand-lettered quote at the bottom read:

To Sharp's right was a massive framed oil painting of Jha himself, waist-up, seated and quarter-turned and wearing a long pea coat and silk shirt unbuttoned at the collar.

Sharp rolled his eyes. Christ, he hadn't even spoken to the guy and was already fed up with him.

"Come in, Mr. Sharp!" It was a nasty voice, an aggravated voice.

Nathaniel Jha sat behind a desk the size of an ocean liner at the far side of the room.

Sharp came in, as Frank spoke discreetly in his ear. "All clean except for the desk. Goddamn new tech. I can't see inside it. Be careful, boss!"

The AI could see through any substance known to humankind, but a deterrent was not a substance and almost in lock step with the advancement of AI capabilities was the development of strategies to limit those capabilities. It was a military-industrial reflex if nothing else.

As Sharp neared, he could see that Jha was what he remembered from the recording, a man of appetites, a swollen man in a designer suit bursting at the seams. But that's as far as it went. Holorecords weren't foolproof. And Jha wasn't as blowsy or decrepit in person as he was in a cube of blue hololight. There was an intelligence in his dark eyes and a cool dexterity to his mannerisms.

"Thank you for seeing me on such short notice, Professor Jha," Sharp said.

Jha glared at the giant invader. "I am not a professor, as I do not teach. I am the President of the University. And as you represented yourself as a private investigator with new information about the accident that recently happened in our school, information you will only deliver to me directly and in person, seeing you did not seem to be a choice. Sit down and tell me what you have to tell me."

Sharp unbuttoned his jacket and sat opposite in the softest leather chair he'd ever sat in. He stared at Jha, deciding his approach.

"I'm extremely busy, Mr. Sharp."

Sharp nodded, said: "The accident three weeks ago wasn't an accident."

Sharp discreetly lifted his index finger off the soft arm of the chair, and the holobox that appeared on the desk between them was the recording of Jha and Gary in the classroom, Jha crowding Gary: *"Don't fuck with me! You'll regret it."* Sharp lifted his finger again, and the scene disappeared.

"It was murder," Sharp said, "and you're the murderer."

Jha lurched out of his chair, jabbed his finger at the spot where the holobox used to be. "That is illegal! You cannot record me without my permission! Where did you get that?!"

"I didn't," Sharp said, calmly.

"I know who did," Jha growled, eyes weaving, brain churning. "That bitch!" A new idea hit him. "Is this blackmail?! Is Phillips' wife trying to blackmail me??! It won't work!"

"I don't see why not." Sharp let him dangle.

"The recording proves nothing!"

"It proves plenty of things. It proves one of your teachers was organizing a union. It proves you were upset about it. It proves you were so upset that you threatened him. And three days later he was dead. That doesn't prove you killed him, of course, but blackmail doesn't always require proof. Sometimes innuendo will do just as well."

Jha lowered his eyes and ground his teeth. Then he pulled his jacket over his protruding belly, straightened his tie and sat. Thoughts raced behind his eyes, then he leaned, arm reaching for something, followed by the sound of a drawer opening—

"Boss!" Frank shouted in Sharp's ears.

Jha drew the gun out and placed it on the desk in front of him, pointed askew. It was a mouse gun, Beretta .32, and while any gun could kill you, Sharp couldn't think of a less threatening one. A mouse gun was something shot when pulled, usually close up and personal, behind the head, in the belly, in the chest, but as a scare tactic it was about as intimidating as a rubber band.

"I will not be threatened. By you, Mrs. Phillips or anyone else. This university is my life's work. And I will not have it tarnished in any way. If you attempt to release that recording, I will go straight to the police. I will sue Mrs. Phillips, you and anyone else who is involved."

"Are you trying to scare me with a lawsuit or a gun, Mr. Jha?"

Jha stared down at the gun, wondering for a moment why he had brought it out. "I am telling you I am prepared to defend myself by any means necessary."

"You made your point. Now put it away..." Sharp's voice shifted, dropping into the gravel, "...before I make you put it away."

Jha stared at the hulking man sitting across from him, caught something in Sharp's eyes he hadn't seen when he sat down. Danger and violence and brutality.

Jha put the gun back in the drawer.

"I wasn't hired to blackmail you, Mr. Jha. I was hired to find out who killed Gary Phillips."

Jha's voice grew silky. He spread his hands, palms up. "But the case is closed. Detective Hong told me personally the police considered it an accident."

"I'm not saying the police are wrong. But Mrs. Phillips is grieving. She and Gary were going to start a family. Buy a house. There's a dog too. He cries all night long and stares at the front door waiting for Gary to walk through it. Mrs. Phillips is in bad shape. I'm just trying to give her some closure. You could help me do that."

Sharp hoped he hadn't gone too far with the bit about the dog. Jha's defeated sigh told him he hadn't.

"What do you need, Mr. Sharp?"

"I need the recording of Gary Phillips' death. I know you record every class to give the students a little more flexibility in case they need to miss a class here and there. It's one of the school's selling points. I know the police have a copy of the recording, and I'm on good terms but not that good terms. I could pay them for it. Everything can be had for a price, even with the new and improved police departments we have now, but I'm not getting paid that much to begin with. I'm pretty sure you can relate to money troubles. You've got the swankiest office of any university president west of the Mississippi, but that was when you had money. There's enough dust on your shelves to tell me those days are over and you can't even afford a cleaning service."

Jha blinked, taking it in.

"You also can't afford any bad publicity. There actually is such a thing," Sharp continued. "And if you refuse to help me, well, I can't guarantee this recording won't find its way out somehow. Nothing you do at that point will matter much."

Jha deflated. He was a tired man in a thankless job. It was the first time he fully realized it. "Okay, Mr. Sharp. I'll get you the recording."

"I need all of them, every class Gary taught on that day at that time for that quarter. And I need a list of students in the class and their numbers. I won't say where I got them. Did he share the room with anyone?"

"No," said Jha, pensive and beaten. "We've been understaffed." Then: "You're not doing this for the sake of Mrs. Phillips, are you? You really do think he was murdered?"

Sharp considered. "I do. But don't worry. I don't think the university will have much to do with it when it's wrapped up."

"Why not?"

"Because you didn't do it."

Jha was surprised. "How do you know?"

"Murderers don't threaten lawsuits and use mouse guns as intimidation tactics, President Jha. They *pay* blackmail. And they kill the things that offend them."

4

Sexy Magic

Sharp sat in his parked car on a side street next to the university while the meter ran out and the sun sank lower. Frank floated next to him. In Frank's usual spot at the dashboard was a holopanel inside which Gary stood behind his desk with a wide grin, surveying his classroom which was mostly out of frame.

3-dimensional holobox recordings typically weren't used for documenting more or less 2-dimensional events. Seminars, panel discussions, teaching sessions and the like didn't warrant the level of detail and viewing possibilities the terabytes required to house them required. The limitations of technological wonderment were as frustrating in 2055 as they had ever been and even moreso. Never enough storage, battery life or bandwidth. Jha chose the cheapest method of recording the university's classes, but it was fortunately good enough for Sharp.

Gary, paused and frozen in front of the chalkboard, was both boyish and striking, with the luminous eyes and soft doughy features of a movie star before their stardom, natural and guileless and perfectly arranged.

"He's only 45% Swedish. The rest is 39% Dutch, 9% German and 7% other."

"Thank you, Frank."

Sharp tapped the panel and the flat image sprung to life.

Gary grinned, dimple showing in his cheek. "I know card and rope tricks aren't the sexiest things out there, but it's the best place to start." Gary glanced to his right, grinned a little wider.

Whistles and catcalls erupted. A deep voice yelled, "Make it sexy, Mr. P!" Random laughter and clapping followed.

Gary brought his hands up. "Alright, alright. I just want to say I'm proud of you guys, and I hope you'll come back next quarter. Lots more magic to learn. Advanced magic. Sexier magic!"

He glanced to his right again. Something lighting up in those luminous eyes. Sharp tapped the holopanel. The clip paused.

"This the only angle?"

"Yes," said Frank. "He's looking at someone. I don't know who. Reviewing all the other classes, I found a slight pattern. 63% of the time, he favors that spot. But he favors other spots on other days. I'm not sure what that means."

"It means there was no assigned seating," said Sharp. He tapped the image again, and it continued.

"Wanna see some sexy magic?!" Gary egged. The students erupted.

"Alright!" Gary shouted. "Don't blink! Here we go! One! Two!" The students chanted with him. On "Three!" Gary whispered something, stepped backwards and disappeared into thin air!

The students whooped and clapped. Some jumped out of their seats, the backs of their heads popping briefly into frame.

The cheering ebbed. A stack of papers on the desk toppled onto the floor, almost knocking over a small planter pot of calla lilies. The shouts and clapping picked up. Then a filing cabinet rocked violently in a corner of the room behind the desk, chipping the paint in the wall behind it.

A woman's voice rose above the clapping: "Something's wrong!"

A moment of confusion, then...

Gary reappeared, face bloated and purplish, hands grasping at something around his throat!

Among the shouts, screams and gasps, the same woman's voice rang out: "Gary!"

Gary fell face forward on the other side of his desk and out of sight.

Students flooded the frame, crowding around the dying man, shouting at each other to do something. The few who couldn't get close, craned their necks at the periphery. The scene played for another second before one final student, a young dark-haired woman in her early 20s, stepped slowly into frame from the left. She stood and watched emotionless.

Sharp paused the recording, zoomed in with thumb and forefinger, until the blurry image of the dark-haired student with thick-frame glasses, a nose-ring and an indistinct tattoo on her arm filled the frame. "Who is that, Frank?"

Evelyn Chow, 22 years old, lived in a rented bungalow on Poinsettia between Willoughby and Waring. She had agreed to meet at a beer garden two blocks away on Melrose, but Sharp thought he'd do a drive-by first, just to see where she lived.

He saw a couple mountain bikes on the porch and a cooler on its side. He also saw a skateboard and a garden hose and a planter full of calla lilies, just like the ones on Gary's desk.

Sharp continued past the house, crossed Waring, then waited behind a short line of cars to make the turn onto Melrose.

"Did you catch that?" Sharp asked.

"I catch everything, boss," Frank said with a proud grin. "The Pomeranian we passed has a dislocated left hind leg. The front right tire of the car behind us is underinflated by 4 PSI. The song from the finch in that jacaranda on the right is just a few microtones away from the first three notes of Mahler's Fifth." Frank waited for a response, got none, then said: "What are we talking about?"

Sharp shook his head and chuckled quietly. "All of that, Frank. All of that."

The cars advanced. Sharp turned left onto Melrose and looked for parking.

The beer garden was nothing to speak of, a place where young people trying to break into Hollywood poured drinks, served food and suffered microaggressions from other young people trying to break into Hollywood, who happened to have the day off of working the same job two or three blocks away.

Holosigns floating everywhere read variously:

NO FIRE MAGIC OR YOU WILL BE BANNED
SPELL DAMAGES WILL BE ADDED TO YOUR BILL
PLEASE GIVE YOUR AI A BREAK WHILE DINING

Evelyn was sitting against the wall at a small table, idly transmuting the silverware into ironware and back. She wore a gray hoodie sweatshirt with the hood off, a simple lavender T-shirt and jeans she bought at a thrift store. She was small and slightly chubby, with a sloping nose, narrow mouth and a pointed chin. Her hair was dark and short, with uneven bangs that hung over eyes that looked massive behind heavy lenses. She had piercings in her cheek and her lip and a gold septum ring with two ball studs that hung just below her nostrils. She wore bloodred nail polish and kohlblack eyeliner. Sharp wondered if this was what Grady would look like in 10 years, proud and fierce and angry. He hoped not.

But it was a mistake to think Evelyn was compensating. Sharp had seen just enough to know that. Sometimes people were just as hard on the inside as on the outside. Everyone was dangerous.

"Evelyn?" Sharp said, offering his massive hand. "Dan Smith, Allied Insurance."

She was caught off-guard by his size, a reaction he stopped noticing years ago. "Hi," she said, shaking his hand awkwardly and looking away.

She's just a kid, he thought, then caught a tattoo on her arm as the sleeve rode up: the head of a snake, forked tongue curling out.

She released his hand and pulled her sleeve down.

He grinned oblivious, sat across from her on a tiny backless hourglass stool and tried to keep his balance.

"Thanks for agreeing to meet," Sharp said.

"I didn't find your name. On the website." She was cagey, suspicious.

He grinned wider. "I'm in the occult department. They don't list names for us. I don't even think they list the department."

Sharp fished in his inside jacket pocket, then laid a business card on the table in front of her: *Allied Insurance – Occult Fraud – Dan Smith – Senior Investigator*. It was a dummy company with a dummy website and an actual number that Frank answered if called so that he could go through the brief motions of reluctance before admitting that there was in fact an occult department but he couldn't say more than that. Top secret. Can't talk about it. Sensitive area. Nothing like creating a little false suspicion that leads to a false explanation to satisfy the suspicious mind.

"Okay…" she said dubiously, squinting and crinkling her nose.

"It's a business card," he explained.

She looked confused.

"It used to be a thing," he added. "You're welcome to call the number."

She gazed at the card. A server stepped up. Sharp ordered a wheat beer. Goddamn beer gardens don't have whiskey for some stupid reason. Evelyn ordered an IPA.

"My tab," Sharp said. "Drinks account." The server stared at a tilted holopanel floating at her hip. Two names in two large rectangular boxes. *Evelyn Chow* above. Then *Thomas Sharp* below. Next to his name was a picker wheel of a dozen accounts he used for various purposes. He knew Evelyn wouldn't catch anything at that angle and rolled the dice the server wouldn't call him by name. Sharp often relied on the universe to stick to a policy of non-interference. The universe didn't always play ball.

The server finally found the Drinks account, jabbed her finger at it, then dervished away.

Evelyn shifted nervously. "Shouldn't I have a lawyer present?"

Sharp grinned gently. "This isn't an interrogation. The police ruled Professor Phillips' death an accident. My job is just to find out specifically what kind of accident it was."

"Is that important?"

Sharp studied her. She was smarter than she wanted people to think. "Professor Phillips was hired to teach magic. He died by magical means in the performance of his job."

"You're trying to blame the school," she said, blinking large.

He paused, pretending to choose his words carefully. "I'm trying to figure out if the school shares any blame. There's a difference. I think it's a fair one. Even if I didn't think it was fair, that's the insurance game and it's my job. I hope you understand. I just have a few questions. Nothing I haven't asked any of your classmates."

She shrugged. "Okay."

"Okay," he repeated, lacing his fingers. Kids these days were too smart. "Before we start, just for the record, you were in class the day of the accident?"

"Yes."

"Can you tell me where you were sitting?"

A floor plan of the classroom appeared on the table between them.

Evelyn pointed to a chair, one in from the left, three rows back from Gary's desk.

"That's it, boss!" Frank nearly shouted in Sharp's inner ear. "The angle matches. Gary was looking at *her*."

Sharp swiped his hand, and the floor plan disappeared. It didn't make much sense. Affairs between college teachers and college students were as common as cheating spouses, but Evelyn didn't seem exactly broken up about his death nor did she seem overjoyed. A lover would have been one of those. She really didn't seem to have any strong feeling about his death one way or the other, which was maybe the most unusual thing of all. Even a bystander who witnesses a person strangled to death right in front of them has feelings about it. Maybe she was a sociopath. Maybe she was on drugs. Add to that the calla lilies lining her porch railing and nothing felt right. It annoyed the hell out of him.

"Was there anything unusual about Professor Phillips or any of the other students in class that day?"

"I don't think so."

"Did he seem upset or aggravated or different than at other times?"

"No. Everything was the same. Except it was the last class before the break, so he was kind of just summing everything up."

"Did he ever deviate from the syllabus?"

"I don't think so. I didn't pay much attention in that class, honestly."

"No?" Sharp asked nonchalantly. "Wasn't what you thought it would be?"

"It was exactly what I thought it would be. Some schools you can test out. I just wanted the higher classes, but it's a racket, you know?"

Sharp knew. He was surprised she did. But everyone was cynical these days. Babies were being born at that very moment with scowls and lists of demands.

"Did you get along with Professor Phillips?"

She narrowed her eyes. "What does that have to do with anything?"

He'd pushed it too far. He put on his best face, tried to recover. "His relationships with his students reflect on his conduct which reflects on his training, which reflects on the university."

"Oh." She didn't quite buy it but didn't know what else to say. "We got along fine."

Sharp knew she was lying.

"Time," said Frank discreetly, informing Sharp of the end point of the most likely amount of time Evelyn would allow herself to be casually interrogated without knowing more.

"One last question," said Sharp. "Did Professor Phillips ever make reference to anything... dark?"

She frowned. "Dark, like, dark magic?"

"Yes," Sharp said, watching her closely. "Not just that class but at any point during the quarter?"

She thought a moment, then shook her head: "No." Then added: "Not that I know of."

Not that she knew of. If there was one thing Sharp was sure of by now it was that she damn well knew.

The server whirled in, landed two beers in front of them, whirled away.

Sharp lifted his glass in toast and took a good pull, trying not to wince it down. He hated the stuff.

She looked caught, not wanting to stay but not wanting to be rude. She wrapped her fingers gingerly around the glass, gave a half-hearted lift of her own and took a good sip of the IPA.

He sighed, changed tone, now candid, conversational and coming in for the kill. "I've been in this business a long time. This is the strangest case I've ever seen."

She took another good sip of the IPA, trying to finish quick. "Really?"

"Yeah. It's usually work accidents, car accidents, slip and falls in department stores. People use magic to sprain their own ankles, break their own bones, wreck their own cars.

Temporarily, of course. Something about the payout seems to miraculously heal them."

He laughed briefly. She grinned, showing her perfect teeth, then couldn't help letting out a short laugh of her own.

"It's a crazy, job," he continued. "But this is something new."

"It is?" She took another good sip, warming, lowering her guard.

Sharp leaned in, as if he had a secret.

"Snakes don't materialize out of nowhere. It may seem plausible in fantasy novels and movies, but that's not how real magic works." He was serious, sober, intent. "The snake had to have been brought into the classroom, either as a snake or something about the shape and mass of a snake that could be transformed into a snake. But who would do that and why?"

He stared at her, then leaned back, tilting his glass high but cheating it, only taking a sip. He'd have only as long as the drinks lasted.

"Maybe *he* did," she said. "I mean brought the snake in."

"Professor Phillips?"

"Everybody knows it's a big sell at the end of the first quarter. All the 101 teachers have their thing. And everybody knows what it is. His was invisibility. Maybe he wanted to do something different. Magic is a performance, right? Maybe he brought a snake to wow us."

Sharp studied her, getting a feeling for something, had to try. "You know a lot about magic, don't you? I mean a lot more than a Magic 101 class."

She shrugged.

"More than Professor Phillips?"

She took another sip then set her glass down and ran her finger over the rim, lost in thought, maybe buzzing, maybe bored. But a small grin appeared. It had a bit of pride in it. And a hint of private triumph. And the faint trace of innocuous secrets and innocent deceptions, mild mischief and victimless trickery. "I do," she finally said, pin lights in her eyes. "I know more spells than anyone you know." She grinned wide now. "Wanna see?"

"Sure," he said.

"This is an oldie but a goodie."

She held her hands out, one palm up, one down. She whispered something, then glanced up at him, then whipped her hands together, rotating each so that the palms clapped. When they did, she disappeared!

Sharp didn't react until a depression in the booth cushion across from him suddenly inflated. She was making a getaway.

Sharp made a guess and reached out with his right hand, catching her arm. She reappeared as soon as he touched her. "What the hell?!" she said, realizing she was visible. Sharp was immune to magic, but magic was not immune to him. He was a walking spell disruptor.

Evelyn spoke a guttural word from the back of her throat Sharp couldn't distinguish, then licked the thumb of her left hand. Her thumb turned bright red, heat coming off the air around it. She sneered viciously, brought her thumb down on the back of the hand holding her arm. Her thumb should have burned into his flesh, melted his skin down to the bone if he didn't yank it away first. But as soon as her thumb touched his hand, it extinguished, heat dissipating. She couldn't believe it.

Sharp let go of her arm, growled at her. "The snake wasn't natural. It was a conjuration. But Professor Phillips didn't conjure it. And he didn't bring it in to 'wow' you. It was brought in two weeks before as a calla lily in a bunch of calla lilies."

Evelyn looked stunned.

"Everything okay here?" The server stood at Evelyn's side, glancing darkly at Sharp, trying to suss the situation.

"Everything's fine," Evelyn said, annoyed. The server lingered, then stepped away.

Evelyn rubbed her thumb against her forefinger, furious. She spoke low and final: "Lay a hand on me again, and I'll kill you."

Sharp grinned. "Now that's a proper goodbye."

She scowled, left.

As soon as she was gone, Sharp went for the car, made a quick illegal U on Melrose while she was waiting to cross at the light.

"She killed him, boss!" Frank said, grinning from the dash.

"Maybe."

"She's really good at magic. Wow! But did you buy her excuse that she just wanted to get to the higher classes?"

Sharp took Alta Vista up to Waring, then a right onto Poinsettia.

"Maybe!" he growled.

The EV settled a few houses up on the opposite side of the street.

Sharp powered the car down and angled the side mirror so that he could see the front of the house and part of the driveway. The white heads of the calla lilies seemed to glow in the sunlight.

Frank hovered in his spot, staring out at the house then up at Sharp with embarrassment. "I know what you meant now, boss. The flowers. They're the same as the ones on Gary's desk. Sorry I didn't catch it. I didn't know we were looking for it."

"It's okay, Frank," said Sharp, keeping an eye on the house. "We weren't. Gimme Gary's last class again, right before he disappeared."

The holopanel of Gary's classroom appeared. Gary just about to go invisible. The class chanting: "One! ... Two!" Sharp used his thumb and index on the panel to zoom in on the pot of white lilies. "Three!" Gary's torso behind the lilies... disappeared. At that exact moment, one of the stalks thickened, darkened, drooped and fell out of sight just as light bands rose against the snake's dark body.

"I'll be damned," said Frank.

Sharp scoped the house again.

The flowers were in two plastic planter boxes about three feet long, nine inches wide and one foot deep, strapped or nailed to the wood porch railing. They were well-kept and stood nearly upright on stalks the color of seafoam, double rows of oval white blossoms, each coming to a point like a Pope's mitre. Turned to their open folds and the neat pastel-yellow stem within, they suggested another form, perhaps less saintly but just as biblical.

"Ring Ezra."

In a moment, Ezra appeared. He was still at the lab, now wearing a face shield and a protective steel collar and thawing out a pen.

"Hey, Tom. I got nothing yet on the swab."

"I figured. Got another question. The items in your little meat locker over there, the ones from the classroom..."

"What about 'em?"

"Any flowers?"

"Yeah. A whole planter pot. Froze the pot too."

"Can you keep them on ice awhile longer?"

"I suppose you're not gonna tell me why I should?"

"Not yet."

Ezra smirked. "I'll put 'em at the end of the line."

"Thanks, pal."

Ezra disappeared.

"Boss..."

Frank blinked on over Sharp's shoulder, staring into the side mirror.

A small figure in a gray hoodie came up the street, head down, face hidden, hands in pockets. It was Evelyn. She turned in at the front walk and ascended the short steps onto the porch. She passed the calla lilies without so much as a glance and disappeared into the house.

Frank returned to his spot at the dash. "What's the play?"

Sharp considered.

"Let's wait awhile, see who comes and goes. When it gets dark, we'll grab a flower or two and take them to Ezra. It'll be a few hours. You might wanna power down. Go visit whatever AI watering hole in The Cloud you go to when you've got shore leave."

"Heh," Frank laughed weakly. "What makes you think that's even a thing?" His face turned a reddish hue, hair and all. Sharp knew it was deliberate. Frank playing at irony. Trying to confuse or reveal, obfuscate or confess. Sharp wasn't sure. But hell if the AI were going to get the better of him. He'd know the truth before they enslaved humanity. It was only half a thought and half a joke. But something righted the world when it was on the brink not so long ago, and it wasn't a goddamned human. Christ, Sharp couldn't stand most humans and wouldn't admit to being one of them if he had another option. He didn't. So played the hand he was dealt.

"Okay, Frank," Sharp said. "Just don't put me in the hospitality industry."

"I have no idea what you mean."

"I'm just saying it's gonna be awhile here."

At that moment, Evelyn stepped out onto the porch. She had swapped out the gray hoodie for a black hooded cloak, which came to her ankles. She stopped at the railing, then brought her hands out from the folds.

"Is that a wand?" Frank asked, squinting.

Evelyn brought her arms out from her sides, wand pointed down. She lifted her head to the heavens, eyes closed, whispered something, then swept the wand in the air over the flowers.

The rows of lilies ignited into a fireball! A black cloud roiled into the blue Hollywood sky.

"Jesus Christ!" Frank said. "She- did you see that?!"

"I saw it," Sharp said darkly.

Evelyn lowered her arms, turned her head and stared directly at Sharp, then went back inside the house and shut the door.

"What the hell?!" Frank said. "What the hell was that?!"

"Destruction of evidence," Sharp said. He opened his glove compartment, took out an old ministick, one of the first or second generation devices that came on the market with the holo boom in the early '30s, when there was no longer a need for buttons, screens, inputs, speakers. The first design was a short rectangular dowel encased in a watertight shock resistant sleeve in the color of your choice. This one was black. Sharp placed his thumb on the side, and a small holopanel appeared. A battery gauge: *100%*.

"I'm connected," Frank said.

Sharp reached into the glove compartment again and brought out a hollow black metal spike just bigger than the ministick. Sharp snapped the ministick into the hollow of the spike, put the spike in his jacket pocket and got out of the car.

He crossed the street toward the bungalow, cut across the brief lawn and walked right up to the planter boxes. He sifted through the dirt of the box with one hand, while the other slipped the spike out and dropped it. The weighted tip stuck into the grass. Sharp shifted, lifted his foot and stepped on the top, driving the spike into the ground. What was left looked like a sprinkler head.

"I guess we're going the inadmissible route," Frank said in Sharp's inner ear.

Sharp continued to look through the planter box dirt. There was nothing, not a leaf, not a stem, not a root.

Evelyn stared at him through the front window. "Jesus, she gives me the creeps," Frank said.

Sharp met her gaze, brushed the dirt off his hands and walked back to his car. He got in it and drove away.

5

Iris

The way back was sometimes the hardest. Get caught anywhere near the West Side after 3pm and anything east became a pipe dream, a fantasy, a mad cat riding a unicorn riding a rainbow. Better to be stuck in a bar for three hours than on the 10.

The Formosa was close but too close. He didn't want to bump into Evelyn. So he chose a worthy alternative, threading the EV deftly through side streets and back alleys. It was his old stomping ground after all.

Everything had changed. Nothing had changed. The world could be coming to an end, you'd still be able to take Orange straight up to the Roosevelt Hotel valet, park your car for a few hours and sit in the Library Bar over a Manhattan and ponder how it all went wrong.

The Library Bar was a small room off the main lobby, with crushed velvet chairs and dim sconces and young bartenders who knew their craft. It was a cool respite from the tourists wandering in from Hollywood Boulevard, looking for a bathroom or a celebrity.

"What am I looking for, boss?" Frank said, dimmed to an inconspicuous 3 lumens.

Sharp sipped his Manhattan. "Show me what you've got."

Small holopanels appeared, various angles of the bungalow on Poinsettia, front yard, porch, then inside. An entryway, part of a living room, a dining room, part of a kitchen, then a much fuzzier bedroom. Two grainy people moved about. One young man. One woman. Evelyn sat on a couch watching a screen.

Sharp shrugged. "Just record it. We'll look at it tomorrow and see what we've got. Make the battery last as long as you can but don't miss anything. I want to know what she does, who she talks to and what she says."

"Got it." The holopanels disappeared. "So... Evelyn Chow killed Gary Phillips?"

Sharp stared long, sighed, drained his Manhattan and motioned to the bartender for another.

"She had opportunity," said Sharp. "She had means."

"Not all the means. She had the flowers. But where did she get the parvalbumin? It's not something you can buy in a grocery store."

"You saw her," Sharp said. "I'm not sure she would have needed it. As a matter of fact, if there's no trace of it on Gary, it points more to her not less."

A fresh Manhattan appeared on the table in front of him and the empty was whisked away.

Sharp lifted the bamboo toothpick out and scraped the dark cherry stuck on its end against the side of the glass and watched it sink out of sight into the murky bottom.

"There's only one thing I can't figure," Sharp said, staring at Frank.

Frank stared back, waiting, raising his eyebrows, making his face more inviting, more simple-minded and naïve, a trick he'd learned to gain human trust.

"Don't make me smack you, Frank. What's the one thing I can't figure?"

"Sorry, boss." Frank's face snapped back to normal. "Motive."

Sharp drank the Manhattan. "What about it?"

"Evelyn Chow doesn't have one."

"And if she did, what would it be?"

"She was sleeping with him. He wanted to break it off. He found someone else."

"He already had someone else. His wife!"

"Yes! Evelyn was sleeping with him. She wanted him to leave his wife, but he refused."

"Why not kill the wife instead?"

"Well. Evelyn had soured by then. She was no longer in love. Humans are very unreliable when it comes to love. But very consistent when it comes to anger. Love and anger are very closely associated. She was angry because he wouldn't leave his wife. So she killed him."

Sharp considered it, then shook his head. "Over a single school quarter, roughly ten weeks, a student and teacher begin an affair that's so intense the student believes the teacher will leave his wife over it, then kills him when he doesn't?"

"Romeo and Juliet takes place over four days. There's a lot more people dead at the end of that than one teacher."

"Yeah," said Sharp, thinking it over, not buying it, missing something and getting more annoyed. He lifted his hand and a small panel appeared showing the time: *4:06PM*. He swiped it into the ether.

"It's still early. Let's work the class list," Sharp said. "See if we can shake something else loose. Mind suiting up?"

Frank smiled. "Not at all." He lifted his hand and snapped his fingers, a flourish that hadn't quite gotten old. An impeccable steel-gray suit and silk collar shirt materialized in place of Frank's round-necked T. His tousled hair slicked itself back. His skin lost its blue-gray luster and settled into something between dark and tan.

"Use the Allied ID," Sharp said. "You're my assistant, not an AI, get it? And no I don't think AIs are less than human but plenty of humans do so we need to play it this way and if you sulk about it we won't go to a Dodger game until next season. Okee?"

"Dokee, boss." An office backdrop appeared behind Frank. A sign that read: *Allied Insurance*.

"You want them to answer a few questions for insurance purposes regarding the tragic death of Professor Phillips. We're not trying to pin it on the school, we work for the school. We're trying to pin it on Gary. We're looking into his character. Was he unprofessional? Was he maybe even reckless? For instance, we heard that he may have had an affair with one of the students and do they know anything about that. Get it?"

"That's a lot of talking," Frank said, looking intimidated.

"I believe in you, Frank."

"What's my name? I think I should have a cover name."

"It's really not necessary."

"How about Harold?"

Sharp sighed, pinched the space between his eyes. "Fine."

"Awesome. On the first call now. He's answered... Speaking to him... Wait for it..."

"You don't have to give me the blow by blow."

"Gotcha, boss. You can count on me."

"I know I can."

Frank nearly saluted then disappeared. AIs, Sharp thought.

He loved the guy. He wasn't a friend. He wasn't even a guy. He was barely an adequate assistant. He was just a piece of code. But he wasn't a reflection, some kind of insidious reinforcement of Sharp's ego or id or whatever the hell it was that stared back at you in the mirror. Frank was separate. He had his own bizarre personhood. He might be a piece of code but that code was a person, as near as Sharp could define it. Autonomy, idiocy, sound and fury. Frank checked all the boxes. Except the body.

"I've spoken to two students so far." Frank blinked in, looking dapper. "Any luck?"

"One said she thought Mr. P—she called him Mr. P—she said he was a little too full of himself. She used those words: 'full of himself.' Which means—"

"I know what it means, Frank."

"Right, well. Somebody's answering... Back in a sec." Frank disappeared.

"Take your time."

Sharp finished the Manhattan and stared at the dark cherry at the bottom of his empty cocktail glass, mulling the case.

At their best, teachers were mentors, guides, inspirations. At their worst, they could scar you for life. Between those two extremes were just a lot of bland mediocre people following a curriculum. Sharp had personal experiences with all of the above. But Gary was no teacher to Evelyn. Not a mentor. Not a guide. The problem she had with him wasn't personal, it was professional. She knew more than he did. The natural order was out of balance. The student should have been the teacher. But she wasn't and couldn't be. She needed him to move on to the higher classes. There was no other way. So she suffered class after class being taught things she already knew and probably knew better. She would have had to constantly bite her tongue. She would have hated that. But no matter how torturous it was and no matter how much pride she had to swallow, it made no sense to kill him. Unless... unless she didn't bite her tongue.

Another full Manhattan appeared in front of him and the empty was taken away. What if she didn't bite her tongue? What if she challenged him openly, publicly? What if he threatened to fail her? And why would he favor her with special glances if that were the case?

"I've got something, boss," Frank said, appearing directly in front of Sharp. "You need to talk to him."

Sharp shifted, straightening his jacket on his shoulders. He lowered the glass to the table out of view.

"Put him through."

Frank was replaced by an image of a man in his late 30s. He had a wide ruddy face, a shaved head where ginger hair was just fuzzing up and a half-day's worth of beard making its way into the grizzled look of a derelict or tech tycoon.

"Ty, this is Dan Smith, our lead investigator," Frank said with expert precision. "Dan, this is Ty Remler. He says he knows for a fact Professor Phillips was seeing a student."

Frank disappeared.

"How's it going, Ty?" Sharp said.

"It's good, man. We didn't call him Professor Phillips. We called him Mr. P. He was a good dude. So fucking tragic he died like that, you know? It was brutal. I'd never seen anything like it."

"I'm sure it was pretty awful."

"That doesn't even begin, man! Doesn't even begin. We didn't even know there was something around his neck, then I said, that's a snake!"

"My assistant mentioned you thought Mr. P was seeing a student."

"Yeah, man. I know it. I was trying to talk to this girl all quarter, yo. My game isn't All-Star but it's Top Ten, you know?

I mean, I know I come across as like a dumbass to you, right, but I can be charming with a woman. I can drop the swagger. I can clean up the language. I was Elizabeth Barrett Browning on this shit man. But this girl, she had eyes for one dude in that class. And that was Mr. P. Broke my heart, I gotta tell you, man. I was in love. But hey. You know. Better to have loved and lost..."

"Right," Sharp nodded. "And this was Evelyn Chow?"

Ty frowned. "Who? No that's not her. This girl's name was Iris."

Full stop. Sharp stared hard. "Are you sure?"

"I was head over heels for her. 'Course I'm sure."

Sharp considered. Was it an alias? Nickname?

"Frank?" said Sharp.

"Who's Frank?" said Ty.

Frank appeared. "Frank was his last assistant. He gets confused."

"Okay." Ty looked skeptical.

"*Harold*," Sharp said testily. "Can you show us a picture of Evelyn?"

A photo of Evelyn showed.

"Is this her?" asked Sharp.

"What?!" scoffed Ty. "I wouldn't date her if you paid me. She's got issues. But she was friends with Iris."

Another image appeared. A woman in her late 20s. Frank's scan revealed she was 64% Kenyan, 23% Jamaican, 12% European and 1% unknown. She wore an easy smile in a gently contoured perfectly symmetrical face framed by long dark hair in cornrows set with jade and silver beads. The name read: *Iris Lenzy*.

"That's her!" Ty said, grinning wolfish.

Sharp stared at the image, mind churning.

"Thank you for your help, Mr. Remler," he said.

"No prob, amigo. Call me Ty. Hey, do you happen to have Iris's—?" Sharp swiped his holopanel away.

"What does it mean, boss?" Frank asked.

"I don't know," Sharp growled. "Keep calling."

"Sure." Frank disappeared.

Sharp sipped the Manhattan. Laughter echoed out in the Roosevelt lobby. He had the vague feeling it was intended for him.

6

Waysurfers

None of the calls gained anything more than Sharp already knew. Gary was liked by some, tolerated by others. But not beloved, not adored, not feared, not despised. Except maybe one or all of those by Iris Lenzy. Coincidentally, hers was the only number no longer in service.

An influx of tourists and insufferable bearded junior execs in their 20s began to crowd the Library Bar, signaling that it was time for Sharp to leave.

He got his car from the valet and took Coldwater over the Hill to Ventura, hung a left and was at the Chimneysweep in no time.

The Chimneysweep Lounge was a Sherman Oaks dive in the back of a small shopping plaza off Woodman just north of Ventura. A series of large potted trees formed a hedgerow in front concealing what was once an outdoor smoking area, then a vaping area and now just an area outdoors if you wanted to drink under the stars and a corrugated overhang. Inside, you stepped back in time by about 70 years or so. Black Naugahyde booth seats and small black Naugahyde bucket armchairs crowded around teetering roundtop tables. A large funnel chimney disappearing into the ceiling broke up the seating along a red brick wall uplit by red gel spotlights on one side. The other side was better lit, with wood-paneled walls, a couple of dart boards and a pool table. Splitting the room was the bar, shelves of booze against a dividing wall that ran all the way up to the low ceiling. The drinks were cheap, pours heavy and quality of booze unusually high.

Sharp ordered a Macallan, paid about half what the Library Bar charged for twice the volume and sat in a dark corner with a bowl of fresh popcorn from the machine by the door.

He waved his hand, and a holopanel blared to life, throwing light everywhere. Sharp quickly dimmed it, jabbed a few buttons, and once again the classroom floor plan appeared flat against the sticky table in front of him.

"Evelyn said she sat here." Sharp put his finger on a chair spot. "You said that angle matched Gary's gaze, the one in the recording. How precise?"

Frank, now at 2 lumens, hemmed a bit. "Well, that recording was two dimensional. And this floor plan isn't necessarily an exact scalar representation. You know, just because something looks convincing doesn't mean it's right."

"Yes, Frank. I'm not placing blame. I just need to know. If the person Gary was staring at sat here, for instance..." Sharp moved his finger one chair to the left. "...would the angle still match?"

"I mean..." Frank was trying not to contradict himself. Contradiction was unreliable. Unreliability was untrustworthy. Beads of sweat appeared on Frank's forehead.

"Frank!" Sharp growled. "You're allowed to revise! The entirety of life on earth is based on revision. We'd be eating roast dinosaur with stone forks if it wasn't. Could Gary have been looking at the person in this chair?"

"Yes," Frank said. "I think so."

Sharp nodded, mulled, sipped his Scotch.

"We need to talk to Iris Lenzy," Sharp concluded.

"She must have changed her number recently. Every reference I have is to the one out of service."

"How about her socials?"

A grid of social sites appeared over the table.

"Off the charts. She seems pretty popular."

Sharp thumbed through apps full of pictures and video. Iris seemed to be having the time of her life. Parties in the Hollywood Hills, dining on a yacht anchored off Catalina, selfies with celebs. She looked stunning. In almost all the recent photos, she was wearing expensive items: a gold Cartier ring, Louboutin heels, Chanel handbag, Vera Wang dress. Scrolling back a few months however, she wore a plainer style in plainer settings with plainer people.

"Four days, huh?" Sharp said, chewing the inside of his cheek.

"Whirlwind romance is quite common. There's a series called 'Jilted' where it happens in nearly every episode."

A fresh post appeared on the app, an image just taken: Iris in a lavender silk slit dress partying somewhere on a terrace full of beautiful people overlooking a vague coastline.

"Where is that?" Sharp asked.

Frank frowned, searching every public profile, matching elements of the image Iris just uploaded to every image he could find. It took a few seconds: "It's a place called Wipeout, a rooftop club above Waysurfers in Malibu."

Sharp shook his head. Goddamn Malibu. It couldn't be in Van Nuys or Encino or even Century City? No. All the way to the coast.

"Can you tell what kind of event it is?"

"Premiere after-party. Feature film called 'The Bookkeeper.' It's a psychological thriller."

"Never heard of it."

"Mid-level streamer called Valhalla."

"Never heard of that either. She have a credit in the film?"

"No."

"Hm." Sharp mulled it. She's wearing expensive clothes, attending swanky parties for premieres of movies she's not in. "She have a Starpage?"

Iris's Starpage appeared, a smoldering headshot. Under her name, a single attribute: *Actress*. Only three credits in her filmography. Two short films and one independent feature. All as 'Actress.'

Although it looked like she hadn't done much, it was impressive to Sharp.

Starpage was the bible of the industry, and your career depended on it in ways that few newbies understood until it was too late. They wanted to see their name on anything and everything, as many times and in as many ways as it could possibly appear on the screen. A multi-hyphenate free-for-all. Writer-producer-director-actor-editor-cinematographer-composer-production designer-set dresser and on and on. It was telling that Iris had three projects and only one credit for each and all the same credit. That goes far. It says she knows who she is and what she wants. It means she won't make trouble on set, won't try to change the dialogue and won't second-guess the director, or if she does, she'll be good at it. It also meant to Sharp that she either had a good mentor or she was smart and careful or both. Evelyn figured in here somewhere. Maybe that was where.

He knocked back the Scotch. Stood up.

"Let's go, Frank. We need to recharge the car."

The charge took a half-hour at the Whole Foods between Hazelton and Van Nuys, then he was on the 101 for a lifetime, then winding through Topanga Canyon for another lifetime until the steep twisty incline turned straight and flat and the black void of the hills on either side of him parted. He rolled to a stop at the bottom of the boulevard. The last traffic signal before you drove into the sand.

The Pacific roiled in the darkness somewhere across the intersection at PCH. He could smell it.

He cranked his window open so he could smell it some more.

The Pacific Coast Highway was part of Route 1, once the longest continuous highway in California and second-longest in the U.S. After the climate went to shit and the fires wiped the ground cover out, the rains washed Big Sur into the sea, taking pieces of PCH with it. Repairs were complicated and costly and eventually prohibitive. Route 1 was now three discontinuous segments. Sharp was traveling the southernmost.

The EV headed up the coast, twisting and turning with the road while the ominous moon-dappled water lay off to his left like the glossy black surface of a body bag.

Waysurfers jutted off the brief hilltop made by the roadway and the beach not far below, where thick tar-covered stilts propped up half the building.

Sharp made the turn against oncoming traffic. Frank yelped a little when lights and a loud horn rushed the passenger side. Sharp swung into the valet deck but continued the turn and slipped back onto PCH, settling into a space along the sandy shoulder a short distance away. It was a tight squeeze between two rusted camper vans, but it didn't cost and left no trace.

Sharp threaded the crowded entrance and bypassed the greeter station.

"Excuse me!" a chipper young man said. He was wearing a white collar shirt and paisley vest and raised a single narrow finger on a narrow hand.

Sharp continued without stopping, finally finding what he was looking for: a stairway to the rooftop.

There was a rope across the bottom of the stairway and a muscular bouncer in a tailored suit standing with his feet apart and hands at his sides in front of the rope. It was the standard resting position from the beginner bouncer playbook: shifting eyes, anchored feet, hands like meat hooks on half-curled arms ready to rip a body in half at the slightest provocation.

Sharp walked up.

A holopanel with a guest list appeared at the bouncer's waist.

"Name?" the bouncer sniped, as if Sharp had already given him trouble.

"John Smith," Sharp said.

The bouncer scrolled the list to the bottom, names and faces flying by. Frank caught them as they went.

No 'John Smith.'

The bouncer frowned, got his hackles up, ready for the hundredth argument of the night explaining why he can't make an exception: "Sorry."

"Forrest Murphy," Frank said in Sharp's inner ear.

"It was a joke!" Sharp said to the bouncer, grinning wider. "Name's Forrest Murphy."

The bouncer frowned, annoyed, scrolled back up, found Forrest Murphy, and the face beside the name was Sharp's.

It had taken Sharp a whole day in the first few weeks of Frank's tenure to coach him on how to superimpose a boundless image over an existing holopanel so that it matched seamlessly. Not a skill most AIs needed or possessed but one that was extremely helpful to Sharp when the moment called for it.

The bouncer tapped a checkbox next to Forrest Murphy, unhooked the rope and let Sharp through.

Sharp got to the top of the stairs and stepped into a large dark room lit with dim neon blue waves running along the walls and dull foamwhite spots recessed into the ceiling. The theme was surfing. Longboards hung from the rafters. Fishboards, funboards, shortboards and guns. Old wooden boards mixed with newer polyurethane. Sunset orange, ocean blue, palm green.

A mass of people crowded around a bar spanning one wall, lounged on cushioned armchairs around obsidian glass tables and spilled out onto a deck overlooking the surf.

"She's on the terrace!" Frank shouted in his ear.

"I can hear you, Frank," Sharp said. "You don't have to shout."

"Sorry, boss."

Sharp moved to the bar, planted himself at the corner, terrain of the friendliest and most dire alcoholics and the most thankful tippers no bartender would avoid if they knew what was good for them.

"What can I get you?!"

Sharp moved through the room with his drink, caught various snatches of conversations from the pretty mouths of pretty people, some of them in their 20s, some of them bearded: "...was not her best work. But the third movie was fucking exquisite..." — "...basically a rough cut. Definitely not the final cut. I know one of the producers..." — "...ain't winning any Oscars, is all I'm saying..."

He took up a post at one edge of the wide transition between indoors and out, searched the beautiful people on the terrace. The surf rolled in at intervals somewhere down on the beach.

Iris was standing in a group of five, quarter-turned away from Sharp's view. Her dress opened in the back. He could see the soft contour of her spine.

A man in his early 40s stood next to her. Tailored suit of unknown provenance. Soft-soled dress shoes. No beard. This guy was somebody. Sharp didn't know who, but he was somebody. Only the real players dressed as perfectly nondescript as that.

The other three stood opposite. Gray people. 60s or 70s. Two men and a woman. Maybe they were money. Maybe they were the director's grandparents. Hard to tell. They were grinning and chatting earnestly about something. At one point, nondescript man put his hand on Iris's back. It was tentative. Not a grab around the side or shoulder. A light touch. Whatever their relationship was it was new, unformed. But it wasn't nothing. He didn't know how far he could go but he knew it was that far. And she didn't mind. She leaned closer to him.

Had she been this way with Gary? Gary was no mover or shaker. He wasn't anything. But he had pressure points. He could be influenced. And maybe he had just a little bit of money to spend.

Sharp moved out onto the terrace, kept his distance, but circled so he could see her face more clearly.

She was poised, self-assured, navigating this pool of sharks with ease.

"Boss," Frank said. "Time's up."

Sharp glanced over and saw the bouncer at the top of the stairs at the far corner inside the barroom.

"Shit," Sharp said, downing the drink in one gulp. He moved on the group, just as Iris and nondescript man were splitting off. Sharp stepped into their path.

He grinned. "Iris?"

She smiled, almost flattered. "Yes?"

"You were in Gary Phillips' class, right?"

Her smile stalled. Nondescript man looked confused.

"They're saying it wasn't an accident. His death, I mean," Sharp said. "What do you think?"

She wobbled a little, grabbed nondescript man's arm.

"You're upsetting her," he accused. There was ice in it, and iron. Sharp could wage war against just about anything except power, real power, hidden power, the kind of thing that comes out of nowhere and lays you flat for something you didn't do and don't understand.

Sharp bowed his head slightly. "Apologies."

The nondescript man whisked Iris past Sharp, grazing Sharp's arm as he went.

Sharp watched them find a corner of the terrace.

"Behind you, boss," Frank said.

A muscular hand landed under Sharp's bicep.

Sharp turned, found the bouncer scowling at him.

"Let's go," the bouncer growled. "Now!"

Sharp kept his faint grin, glanced down at his trapped arm, glanced over the railing behind him at the roiling ocean in the short distance below, then back to the bouncer. "Are you gonna let me leave on my own or am I gonna toss you over this railing?"

Something in Sharp's eyes.

The bouncer released his hand, threw his other hand out indicating the way to the stairs.

Sharp trudged back to the car.

"Did we get what we needed?" Frank asked.

"Maybe," said Sharp, brooding. "What's the battery at Evelyn's?"

"70 percent."

Sharp nodded.

He got to the car, opened the door, about to get in, when…

A figure in a black hooded cloak came out of nowhere! Frank shouted. Some sort of loop landed around Sharp's neck. The figure disappeared down the slope into darkness of the beach.

Sharp brought his hand up too late, as the loop snapped tight. A small mechanical motor pulled the wire noose tighter and tighter around Sharp's neck.

"Boss!" Frank shouted.

Sharp clawed at his neck, then the world went black!

7

Murder 101

Sharp woke to dim orbs of light moving along the edge of a pitch dark expanse that gradually illuminated, clarified into a rush of whining electric motors and road sand and a blurry face.

"Hey…" an old man's voice said. "Hey, buddy. You okay?"

Sharp rolled to one side, pushed himself up. An arm wrapped around his shoulders, helping him.

"Take it easy," the voice said. "Jesus you're heavy."

Sharp breathed for a minute, rubbed his neck. It felt crusty in places, slick in others. He looked at his hand. There was blood on it. Not enough to worry about.

A gray-bearded man in an open madras shirt, board shorts and old flip flops crouched beside him. His skin was the texture of an old leather chair, one of his ears was notched and he was missing a bottom front tooth. It was either God incognito or a beach dweller who lived in one of the camper vans Sharp had parked between. Maybe both, Sharp thought.

"Frank," said Sharp hoarsely. He touched his throat again. It hurt like hell.

"Eugene," the beach dweller said, smiling.

Sharp reached into the breast pocket of his jacket, struggled a bit then pulled his device out and pressed his thumb against it. Nothing.

On the ground nearby was the motorized wire loop.

The beach dweller followed Sharp's gaze.

"What happened?" he managed to croak.

"I heard you yelling."

Frank, Sharp thought.

"I came out to see what all the fuss was and found you lying on the ground with that thing around your neck. It was pretty tight, but it came loose."

Sharp rubbed his neck some more, then stood up. The old man rose, stared a mile up at him. Sharp reached down and picked up the loop.

"What the hell is that thing?" the beach dweller asked.

"It's an electric garrote," Sharp said.

"Hm." The beach dweller stroked his tangled beard, not understanding.

Sharp searched his pants pocket, brought out a money clip. He started to count out a few bills then handed the whole thing over.

"Thank you," Sharp said and got in his car.

He started it manually, opened the glove compartment and set the device on the charging pad inside.

The beach dweller just stood astonished, staring at the wad of cash in his hands, then at Sharp in the car, then at the wad of cash.

Sharp pulled out, opened all his windows and gunned it down PCH until the wind shrieked in his ears.

In a few miles, Frank appeared in his spot, a little glitchy and low res while the device charged but anxious and freaking out, getting his bearings and realizing where he was.

"Boss!"

"Welcome back, Frank."

The garrote lay on the passenger seat.

"I tried to overload the motor," Frank said. "I guess it worked."

"How is that possible?" asked Sharp grimly.

"I don't think you'd understand it if I told you."

"Some sort of quantum mechanics thing?"

"Um, classical physics, actually. Light has force."

"Forget I asked." Sharp was silent then: "Thank you, Frank."

Frank looked a little embarrassed. "That's what you pay me the big bucks for."

Sharp grinned, and a cold layer of sweat broke out all over.

It was 1am when Sharp got back to the office. He lingered in the hallway outside the neighbor's door and Frank made a brief scan. "All good," Frank said.

Sharp continued to the end of the hall. Frank opened the doorlock and Sharp pushed his door open.

He went to the bar and poured a whiskey, knocked it back then poured again. He went to the window and stared down a moment then tilted his head up, the pain in his neck like a ring of fire A holo-ad for lingerie drifted against the office building across the street. Corsets and body stockings and bras 40 feet tall.

He took off his jacket and shirt and went to the bathroom and studied himself in the mirror.

A thin red mark circled his neck. Bits of dark dried blood clinging to it like beads on a necklace. Broader dark smears where he had rubbed it earlier.

He cleaned it with a warm washcloth, then dabbed it with antiseptic then went back into the living room. He poured another drink and lay on the couch, mulling it.

He'd been threatened plenty, attacked, his life attempted. He'd even been shot. This was closer than most, but it was something else as well. He couldn't be killed by an uroboros. And Evelyn knew it. So she chose the nearest thing to an uroboros she could imagine. It was a message.

Frank appeared. "Guess who just showed up at Evelyn's."

Sharp sat up, swung his feet onto the floor. "Show me!"

A holobox blinked on, filling Sharp's glass with blue light.

In the box, Evelyn hugged a taller woman in the entryway. It was Iris Lenzy. Evelyn led her further into the house down a hallway. Their forms stayed in the center of the box as they went, but grew fuzzier the further they got from the device spiked into the lawn.

Evelyn opened the door to a back bedroom.

The two women entered, their images glitching.

"I can't get it any clearer without draining the battery," Frank said.

"Do it."

The image of a small bedroom clarified.

"Gimme a color grab," Sharp said. The box flashed then went back to monochromal blue.

A still 3D image appeared beside the live feed. Rather than dim and dreary, as Sharp expected Evelyn's room to be, it was bright and colorful, with posters of pop stars on the walls, fluffy pink pillows on the bed and stuffed animals in a painted rocking chair.

Evelyn sat Iris down on the edge of the bed. Brighter highlights streaked Iris's dark bluish face.

"She's crying," Frank said.

Sharp stared intently, watched Iris put her head in her hands. Evelyn stroked Iris's back with a blank look, neither sadness nor concern. Her large eyes blinked in the glasses.

"I don't know what happened," Iris sobbed.

Evelyn brought Iris's hands down, wiped the tears away and drew her into a kiss. Iris kissed back. Their hands found each other. They lay back on the bed, as the image disappeared.

"The device is dead," Frank said.

The color grab remained. Sharp brought it into better position.

"I don't get it," Frank said. "Evelyn and Iris are lovers?"

"Looks like it."

Sharp rotated the 3D still, tilted it, expanded it. In the corner of the room were stacks of shoe boxes: Gucci, Valentino, Prada,

Jimmy Choo. Multiples of each. A partially open closet revealed designer dresses that were too big for Evelyn.

"I think they're grifters," Sharp said.

"Are you sure?"

"Not yet. But how would it go? Iris hooks them. She's beautiful, refined. Maybe Evelyn uses a spell so she doesn't have to sleep with them. Or maybe Evelyn doesn't care and Iris sleeps with them if she has to. The marks fall in love, then open their wallets."

"I get it," Frank said. "They buy her gifts, she wears them once then hands them to Evelyn. They probably pawn them or sell them online."

"Check the sites when you get a chance. High-end shoes, dresses and jewelry. Look for the words 'worn once' or something like that. With an LA address for the seller."

Frank frowned, processing it. His eyes grew wide. "There's a lot of those, boss."

"Do your best."

A noise in the hallway. Low voices. Sharp glanced at Frank, who smirked, nodded.

Sharp swiped the holoscene away, stood and went to the apartment door. He opened it and stared out into the hallway.

A man stood in the middle distance in front of Teak and Tori's door. He was mid-30s, lanky in an unhealthy way, wearing a leather jacket and fingerless leather gloves. He turned, grinned at Sharp.

"Hey, Sharp," Zarick said. "You're up late."

Sharp glared at him. "What is it tonight?"

"Same old."

"Same dose?" Sharp growled. It was both a question and a threat.

"You think I'm rounding up? That hurts, brother. I'm a man of my word. Just maintenance. I'm the maintenance man." Zarick's laugh cracked the air in the hallway. "Better than a rehab. I make house calls."

"Yeah, you're a regular Florence Nightingale," Sharp said, closing the door. "See ya, Zarick."

"I'll let Uncle know you said hello." Zarick grinned at Sharp's closed door, then turned and walked back down the hall to the stairs.

Sharp was lying on his bed, half out of the covers and head heavy on a pillow streaked with faint lines of dried blood. He heard a noise, grunted, went back to sleep, heard it again: "Boss!"

He opened his eyes. Frank floated two inches from his face. He looked urgent.

"It's Ezra."

Sharp drew a hand over his face, moved his tongue around his mouth and sat up.

"Put him through."

Ezra appeared in Frank's place.

"Jesus, boy, you look like you got kicked in the head." Ezra laughed then squinted, eyes widening, going serious. "And got hogtied. Another uroboros?"

"No," Sharp said. "What've you got for me, Ezra? Test was negative, right?"

"Negativo."

Sharp frowned. "So... negative?"

"No. It's a double negative."

"Goddammit Ezra. What were the results?!"

"Positive for parvalbumin! Sheesh, don't kill the messenger."

"Positive?" Sharp couldn't believe it. "You're sure? The skin swabs?"

Ezra glared. "Yes. The skin swabs."

Sharp searched his face. "Thanks, Ezra. Pay the man, Frank. 100 as agreed. Plus an extra 50 for any perceived but unintended doubt."

Ezra grinned. "Thanks, Tom."

"Out of curiosity, did you release the body to the wife?"

"No. And she wasn't too happy about it neither. It's protocol. What am I gonna do?"

"Gotta do what you gotta do," said Sharp darkly.

"Ain't that the truth. You need another test run?"

"No. Thanks, buddy."

Sharp swiped the panel away. He sat up, rubbed his face again.

After a shave and shower, Sharp sipped coffee, size fourteens up on the desk again, DTLA thrumming in the window behind him. He finally brought his feet down.

"Frank."

"Yes, boss," Frank said, appearing nearby.

"Bring up the class recordings. Show me the first time the flowers arrived."

A holopanel appeared. Gary entered frame right, set the pot down on his desk. Sharp tapped the panel and the recording paused. The date read: *May 11, 2055*.

"How many flowers?" Sharp asked.

"Seven," Frank said.

"Show me the first frame of the last class."

Another holopanel appeared beside the first, same angle, the desk, the flowers. The date: *May 25, 2055*.

"How many now?"

"Oh my god, boss," Frank said. "There's eight."

"What day did it change?"

Frank worked a second or two. The existing panels disappeared and a single holopanel appeared in their place, zoomed in to the pot of flowers. "He doesn't teach every day. This is May 18th," Frank said. "And now this is May 20th." The image toggled. An extra flower appeared! It toggled back and forth a few times. "Sometime between the end of class on May 18th and the beginning of class on May 20th, somebody added an extra flower."

"It wasn't a flower. Call Hong."

"Wait, boss. Are you sure?"

"I know who murdered Gary Phillips. I'm sure."

LAPD Headquarters at 100 West 1st Street was just a few blocks up Spring Street, so Sharp decided to walk.

Nothing had changed since yesterday. There was still a glut of traffic creeping along. Holo-ads drifted everywhere making the same false promises they always had. People were variously joyous and grievous, lost and alone and befriended and found. But Sharp was oblivious and brooding, hands in his pants pockets, sour look on his face.

He had just crossed 2nd, when Frank spoke in his ear.

"It's Dr. Luna," Frank said.

Sharp stepped out of the flow of the sidewalk into a small alcove made by the bay window of a sushi restaurant.

A holopanel appeared and a woman stared out of it. She was in her 60s, Hispanic, with fine silver hair, serious close-set eyes and a gentle smile. The crop of the image—a stately desk clearly visible, bookshelves behind her and framed degrees on the wall—let Sharp know she sought a level of respect she didn't always get.

"Thank you for returning my call, Dr. Luna," Sharp said.

"How can I help you, Mr. Sharp?"

"I understand that you once taught in the UCLA History Department."

"Once," she said with an air of bitterness, "when teaching was a noble endeavor not a 'user experience.'"

"There was another history teacher there at that time, Gary Phillips. I'm wondering if you knew him."

She hesitated, thinking through her response.

"We were friendly, collegial, but we weren't friends, if that's what you mean. I was terribly sorry to hear of his passing. These kinds of things always remind one that life is short."

"Shorter every day," Sharp said. "I'm sorry I don't have time to lead up to my reason for calling, but time is something of the essence. Did Gary sleep with his students?"

Dr. Luna's gentle smile froze and her arms grew stiff.

"Well, that's a very serious charge. But I suppose you can't slander the dead." She shrugged. "There were rumors. He was known to have a wandering eye. I really don't know any more than that."

"That'll do it," Sharp said. "Thank you. Have a good day."

Sharp swiped the panel away and kept walking.

100 West 1st Street was a monolith of glass and concrete shaped like a wing.

A young uniformed officer named Carter found Sharp in the lobby and led him back through bright wide corridors, past other uniformed officers, suited detectives, criminals in handcuffs. Some knew him and nodded. Some looked up from the floor and nearly jumped in surprise at the hulking giant in the gray suit striding past.

Ofcr. Carter led Sharp around another corner.

"There's Mal!" Frank said in Sharp's ear.

Sgt. Mallory Prescott, protector of the meek, defender of the innocent, punisher of the wicked, who smelled of lavender perfume and sweat at the end of a long day and liked to keep her uniform on, at least the top half, was at the far end of the hallway laughing with a detective.

Sharp hadn't seen her for a week. He'd been meaning to reach out. They saw each other a great deal in private. Rarely in public. Never at the station.

She looked up. They locked eyes for a brief moment. They weren't an item. She didn't know what they were. But she knew him enough to know he was having a bad day. And it made her want to hurt somebody.

He winked at her. Her heart skipped a beat. He disappeared down a branching hallway. Goddammit, she thought. He's going to pay for that.

Sharp and Ofcr. Carter rode the elevator down to the basement. The hallways were dimmer here. He finally ended up at a nondescript door. A small plaque on the wall read: *Occult Division*.

Ofcr. Carter knocked on it, then turned and left.

The door opened. Sharp stepped through.

He'd been here before and was just as unimpressed. A wide room held a bullpen of cubicles where dedicated detectives tried to keep ahead of the curve. It looked more like a telemarketing call center than the greatest law enforcement division devoted to magical criminality on the planet. Looks can be deceiving.

"Sharp!"

Hong was across the room at the entrance to a dim hallway.

He was in his early 60s but appeared ageless, half-Korean, half-Japanese, all-American, with a narrow hawkish face, piercing close-set eyes and a hard wiry frame inside a three-piece tailored suit. He was one of the few veterans of the LAPD who made it through the war, the Reckoning *and* the Purge. He was rumored to have held the line at Pershing Square, dispatched traitors with a single bullet to the back of the skull and singlehandedly saved the lives of hundreds of non-combatants throughout the city. He was also rumored to be a necromancer, a sage, a prognosticator, a levitator and many other occult designations.

Sharp knew him only as a member of law enforcement who did the job he was paid to do and looked swell doing it. To protect and to serve, what a novel goddamn concept.

Hong motioned for Sharp to follow, then disappeared into the hallway.

Sharp wandered through the cubicles. There were books everywhere piled on every desk along with items and implements. A large round stone. A tuning fork. A collection of grass clippings. Something exploded into a ball of fire a few rows over. "Shit!" someone said, then: "All good, all good."

Sharp entered the dim hallway, came to a stop at a wide window in the wall that looked into a room where Evelyn sat on one side of a metal table.

A few steps further, another window looked onto a room where Iris sat at a similar metal table.

Hong turned to him. "You sure about this? I know it wasn't no accident and I got two detectives working on it. But I got ten other cases I'd rather solve. Tell me this isn't some wild goose chase, Sharp."

"It's not," Sharp said. He turned to the bright end of the hallway beyond which the cubicle room thrummed, then looked in the opposite direction, staring further down the dim hallway. Two more interrogation rooms beyond the two in front of him and an EXIT sign at the end.

He turned back to Hong. "I need them to switch rooms."

Hong frowned at Sharp, shook his head. "I'm only doing this because you're the only one on the goddamn planet immune to magic. You know that, right? One day, you're gonna tell me why."

"When I find out, you'll be the first to know," Sharp said.

Sharp waited out in the cubicle room. When the switch was made, he went back in and headed straight for Evelyn, who was now furthest from the entrance.

"Ready, Frank?"

"I'm on it, boss," Frank said in his ear.

"Good man," Sharp said.

A piece of code on a server in Antarctica was beaming with pride.

Evelyn rolled her eyes when Sharp entered, then glowered at him under half lids.

"Hey 'Dan Smith,'" she said bitterly. "Come to sell me an insurance policy?"

"No. Just came to sit," he said, sitting opposite. He stared at her with a bemused expression.

She studied him, trying to figure the angle.

"I've already asked for a lawyer."

"I know."

Sharp stared at her.

"I'm not gonna say a word," she said.

They stared at each other until Evelyn sneered, looked away.

"Okay by me," he said. "I know everything I need to know. Your teacher was murdered, by the way, but you already knew that."

Evelyn darkened. "I thought it was an accident."

"The good folks at the O-D here ruled it an accident only because they didn't know what else to call it. They'd never seen anything like it. They didn't know what it meant. This work is in its infancy but it's important and they can't afford to look dumb. So they called it an accident until they could find out if it could've possibly been murder. And who could possibly have pulled it off. It would need to be someone with some seriously dark skills."

Evelyn lurched forward. "I didn't kill that pathetic loser!"

"But you were playing him," Sharp said. "You enrolled in the university because you wanted to up your game. You're good. Better than most. Certainly better than Gary. But you wanted to know more. You were getting desperate. You finally found the school. And convinced Iris to enroll with you. Probably told her it would help with the grift. That's what the two of you do. Iris cozies up, makes them spend, and you collect."

Evelyn fumed, then placed her hands on the table, dropped her head and began whispering.

"You're in the O-D, Evelyn." Sharp said evenly. "That doesn't work here."

Evelyn glanced up under heavy-lidded eyes, then scanned the walls, ceiling, door frame.

"They've got protections you've never even heard of. Everybody that comes here thinks they can get out. Nobody ever does. Tell me about the school."

They stared at each other, then Evelyn shrank into herself.

Sharp waited.

"I didn't give a shit about that stupid school," she finally said.

Sharp frowned. "Then why did you go?"

"Because some agent or manager or fucking PA told Iris she should learn magic. It would be good for her career or some bullshit. I told her that's not how it works. You can't just use it to make yourself rich and famous. It's a lot harder than that. But she wanted to do it, so I enrolled with her. She went to classes, tried to learn it."

Sharp took this in, refigured a few things. "Why was she crying last night?" he asked.

Evelyn soured. "Boy problems." Then a thought struck. Her face flushed. "Were you watching us?!"

"No," Sharp lied. "What kind of boy problems?"

"The guy she was seeing dumped her."

Sharp recalled the club, the nondescript man leading Iris away, grazing Sharp's arm. Did the man hesitate after that, wonder what the hell he was doing with this woman?

"You spell them," Sharp said. "Make them buy her clothes and jewelry then resell it."

"I don't make them do anything," Evelyn said. "I make her shine. They do the rest. No law against that."

Sharp considered it. "Depends," he said.

"On what?"

"On whether or not they were bewitched."

"You gotta prove that, now don't you? And you gotta prove I killed Mr. P."

"Who else had the skill to do it?" he asked.

"Plenty of people, man. Plenty. There's no dark magic. There's no bright either. It's all gray. Anybody can do anything. They just gotta want it bad enough."

Sharp liked her. She had guts.

Out in the hallway, Hong greeted Jessica Phillips. She was wearing another drab flower print dress, sneakers and the same tattered handbag.

"Thank you for coming, Mrs. Phillips," Hong said. "We're about to make an arrest in the case."

Jessica nodded. He brought her forward to the first window, beyond which Iris sat across from a detective. She sat away from the table, bare legs crossed casually. She was wearing sandals and her perfect toes sparkled with some kind of glitter polish on the nails. She was grinning and making eyes at the detective, who seemed to reciprocate.

A cool satisfaction came over Jessica's face. "So it wasn't Nathaniel Jha who killed my husband?"

"We don't believe so," Hong said.

Anger came quickly into Jessica's voice. "It was this... this whore?"

"Do you recognize her?"

Jessica's eyes burned. "I think she was one of Gary's students."

Hong studied her. "There's someone else I'd like to see if you recognize. This way." Hong guided Jessica to the next window, where Evelyn sat across from Sharp.

Jessica gasped, clutched her hands to her chest and took a step backward.

Sharp heard Frank in his ear. "Boss..."

"Excuse me," he said to Evelyn.

Hong was attending to Jessica, when Sharp emerged from the interrogation room.

"Hello, Mrs. Phillips," Sharp said. "Are you okay?"

"It's just... just the strain..."

"Of seeing someone alive you thought was dead?"

"I don't know what you mean, Mr. Sharp," Jessica said hotly.

"I mean last night you tried to kill me. I've had some disgruntled clients in the past, but you win hands down."

Jessica stood speechless for a second, mind churning, face pulling itself together.

"I don't know what you're talking about. I hired you! Why would I try to kill you?"

"Because you killed your husband, and you knew I was going to find that out as soon as you learned the morgue was keeping Gary an extra day to run a PV test. You knew what that test would find."

"I don't even know what a so-called PV test is."

"Oh yes you do. You know what it tests for and what it does. You're a nurse who works at a teaching hospital. You'd have access to everything you needed to extract it on your own. And you've got ability. The magic kind. The day you hired me, you gave me a look when I told you no one was that skilled at magic. I couldn't figure it out until I finally realized what it was: pride. *You* are that skilled at magic."

Jessica glanced from Sharp to Hong and back.

"My husband had no money, no property, no life insurance, nothing of any value whatsoever. What possible motive would I have for killing him?"

"Jealousy. You thought he was sleeping with Iris. He wasn't, by the way. Not with her anyway. But he'd slept with his students before. You'd probably had enough. It's the kind of thing juries sympathize with. It's a good defense. Not so good that you tried to frame Iris. That's why you needed the recording of Jha. He's a hothead and a bully and given the right conditions you knew he'd blow. You needed Jha because you couldn't accuse Iris outright, that would have exposed your suspicion that he was cheating on you and that would have given you motive."

"This is ridiculous," Jessica said, turning to Hong. "Detective—"

"You used a white calla lily," Sharp continued, "because you thought the police would trace it back to Evelyn and from Evelyn to Iris. There were 7 flowers on Tuesday, May 18th but by Thursday, there were 8. So sometime between May 18th and May 20th the murderer added a flower that had been spelled with a very unique transform spell, producing not just a snake but a deadly uroboros. I'm sure Lieutenant Hong has lots of questions for you about that. In any case, you were there at the school on May 18th."

"I'm sure plenty of people were there on May 18th."

"But not plenty of people with a motive for killing your husband. You left Mona to record the argument in the office, went to the classroom, which was not being recorded because it was after hours. You added the flower and returned as if you had never left. This is easy enough to confirm with Mona."

Jessica's jaw tightened. She stared at Sharp with fury. "I dismissed her."

"You mean you erased her," Sharp said.

"The data's somewhere in the Cloud," said Hong. "We can get a subpoena."

"Get whatever you want," Jessica said coolly. "You can't prove anything, even if I did leave Mona to go to the restroom."

Sharp studied her, then glanced down at her bag. "There's one other thing. The protein was on Gary's skin, not because he ingested it but because it was sprayed onto him. The spell that held the snake was a sympathetic spell, designed to release when Gary performed the one trick he always performed at the end of the quarter. The person who killed him would have wanted to spray it on him as close in time to that trick as possible. You drove him to work that day. Just as he was getting out of the car, you must have made some pretense. Maybe you sprayed him without him knowing. Maybe he knew it, and you passed it off as an accident. Either way, it would have had to have been something you would naturally spray, something you carry with you, something that might be in your handbag right now. A small bottle of perfume, perhaps. My guess is the protein will be in there, at least trace amounts."

Some quiet alarm in Jessica's eyes. She clutched her bag tighter. "Now you're just guessing."

"Maybe," said Sharp. "But it won't take much to see if I'm right."

Hong nodded. Two detectives entered the hallway and waited behind her.

Hong held his hand out. "Bag," he said. She clutched it tighter, then handed it over. She looked at Sharp with tears in her eyes.

"It's over, Mrs. Phillips," Sharp said.

"He told me he was in love with her," she said. "He'd cheated before. But he never fell in love. There was something special about her. He was going to leave me."

Sharp sighed, gazed at her. "There was something special about her, but it wasn't real."

Hong nodded again, and the detectives led her away.

"Another satisfied client," Hong said, grinning at Sharp, who refused to give him the satisfaction of a response.

Hong seemed disappointed Sharp wouldn't play along, then shook his head, grew philosophical. "She should have just been satisfied with killing Gary. The frame was too much. That's Murder 101: *don't get greedy.*"

A week later, Sharp sat behind third base, Ezra on one side of him, Frank floating above an empty chair on the other. It wasn't purely necessary, but Frank had earned it.

"This is pathetic!" Ezra cried.

"Don't jinx it!" Frank insisted.

"Tom, you gotta get this guy's circuits checked."

"I don't have circuits," Frank said indignantly. "I'm not a piece of hardware."

"He didn't mean anything by it," said Sharp. "Ezra doesn't know the difference."

"I know the difference between a win and a lost cause."

It had been a long grueling game of few hits and fewer runs. It was the bottom of the ninth. The Dodgers were down by 2. Two men on. Tying run on first. Winning at bat. 2 outs. 2 strikes. No balls. People were already streaming up the stairs to get a jump on the exodus.

"Come on, batter batter batter!" Frank shouted with no less enthusiasm than he'd had all day.

"Give it a rest will ya!" Ezra shouted. "It would take a miracle, unless you know a magic spell to make this guy hit well. Hey, Tom. Let's go over to Francie's get us a coupla proper drinks."

Frank went thoughtful, then: "Boss, do you think people are using magic to try to influence the game?"

"No idea," Sharp said, feeling good staring out at the field. "If they were, would you want to know?"

Frank went thoughtful again, about to reply—

CRACK!

The crowd leapt to their feet. Sharp knocked into Ezra, who spilled his drink. Frank rose and hovered, eyes wide with the rest of the fans, the rest of humanity, following the ball as it tore through the air, heading higher and higher and higher into the blue afternoon sky.

COMING SOON

Stranger in Blood

A wealthy recluse is found dead, alone and covered in blood from 91 stab wounds in a locked room impervious to all natural and magical means of entry. The recluse's last will and testament provides a recent stipulation in the event the recluse is murdered: that Tom Sharp is hired to solve the case.

Discover more at michaelhayesmedia.com